'Was giving m[e ...] idea?'

When he said no, [...] your conscience? You couldn't feel you owed me?'

'Owed you for what?'

'For moving Nigel out of my life. You did do that?'

'I did.'

'In his best interests, of course.'

She made that heavily sarcastic, and Nicolas drawled, 'Well, it doesn't seem to have done you much harm.'

Rage was blurring her sight and her speech. She said raggedly, 'It could have finished me, for all you cared.'

Dear Reader

As spring moves into summer, you can't help but think about summer holidays, and to put you in the right frame of mind this month's selection is jam-packed with exotic holiday destinations. As a tempter, why not try Patricia Wilson's new Euromance, DARK SUNLIGHT, set in sultry Spain? *And*, who knows, you may well find yourself one day visiting the very places mentioned in the novel! One thing's for sure, you're bound to have lots of fun on the way...

The Editor

Jane Donnelly began earning her living as a writer as a teenager reporter. When she married the editor of the newspaper she freelanced for women's mags for a while, and wrote her first Mills & Boon romance as a hard-up single-parent. Now she lives in a roses-round-the-door cottage near Stratford-upon-Avon, with her daughter, four dogs and assorted rescued animals. Besides writing she enjoys travelling, swimming, walking and the company of friends.

Recent titles by the same author:

THE TRESPASSER

HOLD BACK
THE DARK

BY

JANE DONNELLY

MILLS & BOON LIMITED
ETON HOUSE 18-24 PARADISE ROAD
RICHMOND SURREY TW9 1SR

All the characters in this book have no existence outside the imagination of the Author, and have no relation whatsoever to anyone bearing the same name or names. They are not even distantly inspired by any individual known or unknown to the Author, and all the incidents are pure invention.

All Rights Reserved. The text of this publication or any part thereof may not be reproduced or transmitted in any form or by any means, electronic or mechanical, including photocopying, recording, storage in an information retrieval system, or otherwise, without the written permission of the publisher.

This book is sold subject to the condition that it shall not, by way of trade or otherwise, be lent, resold, hired out or otherwise circulated without the prior consent of the publisher in any form of binding or cover other than that in which it is published and without a similar condition including this condition being imposed on the subsequent purchaser.

*First published in Great Britain 1993
by Mills & Boon Limited*

© Jane Donnelly 1993

*Australian copyright 1993
Philippine copyright 1993
This edition 1993*

ISBN 0 263 78037 6

*Set in Times Roman 11 on 11½ pt.
01-9306-49669 C*

Made and printed in Great Britain

CHAPTER ONE

'LOOK at this!' shrieked Clarry Rickard, to her staff of one elderly man. The letter that had arrived with the bills in this morning's mail was certainly impressive.

With an embossed address 'King's Lodge', someone signing himself 'Paul Burnley, estate manager' was telling them that an Elizabethan manor had items including several period chimney-pieces needing attention. If Miss Rickard felt that her team could handle the repair restoration he would be pleased to discuss the matter.

Clarry tapped the number and waited, listening to the ringing. When a man said, 'Speaking,' in answer to her query she said, 'Clare Rickard here. I've had your letter, and I'm very interested. Could we come down tomorrow and see what your requirements are?'

The estate manager said he looked forward to meeting her, and they talked a little about the history of the house. Then she asked, 'Who owns it?'

'The Strettons have lived here since the late forties,' he told her. 'But it was recently taken over by Dargan Enterprises. Nicolas Dargan—you may have heard of him.'

It hit her like a punch in the stomach, driving the breath out of her so that it was a few seconds before she could say, 'May I call you back? Something has just come up.'

She put down the phone and raised a set white face to Danny. 'Cole Dargan owns King's Lodge,' she said flatly.

A silent man was Daniel Hill, master craftsman and taciturn to the stage where some who had known him for years had hardly heard him talk at all. He said nothing now, but he looked as though there was a bitter taste in his mouth.

'I can't work for him!' Clarry wailed, running a hand through her mass of dark chestnut hair, in which a white streak made a dramatic contrast. 'Why should he choose us?'

'Who says he did?' said Danny, and indeed, a tycoon like Nicolas Dargan would hardly be bothering with small details such as who was doing minor repairs on his properties.

They could certainly use the work. Clarry was managing to pay the rent on workroom, storage and office space in an industrial unit, and a living wage for herself and Danny. But this sounded like a prestige job that could lead to all manner of things as well as being a delight to do.

She recalled the number and said, 'Sorry about that. Tell me, who's living there?'

'The staff, of course. And the Colonel and Miss Stretton are staying for the time being. But we could accommodate your workers if it would be more convenient.'

'That sounds lovely.' She used her husky voice that customers seemed to like. 'And will Nicholas Dargan be there?'

'No, you'll be dealing with me.'

'We'll be with you about midday, then. And I'm sure we can handle the work, it sounds exactly the kind of thing we specialise in.' As she put the phone down again the tip of her tongue ran between dry lips and she had to swallow before she could say, 'Nicholas Dargan won't be there.'

Danny grunted, and Clarry thought, it has to be over a year since I said his name, and it still hurts my throat to get it out.

When Clarry turned her van through the wrought-iron gates in the ivy-covered wall and saw King's Lodge it was just about perfect. Not one of your sprawling great manors but a gem of a house, with its gables and tall chimneys, the diamond-paned windows keeping their secrets, each room with its own story.

She would have envied anyone who lived here, but only in a cheerful lucky-for-some way, not with this seething resentment. That was because it was the property of Nicholas Dargan, and to him it would be just another investment. It seemed wrong that he should be master of a house so beautiful that it sent her misty-eyed.

She stopped the van and got out, and almost at once the man she had spoken to on the phone came out to meet her. She had arrived on time in a van painted dark blue, with 'Rickard Restoration' in gold script on the side. So he hardly needed to ask if she was Miss Rickard. But he did, shaking her hand and holding it rather longer than necessary.

Men were usually pleased to meet her, because she was a striking girl, with grey-green eyes over high delicate cheekbones, and a full sensuous mouth that sometimes gave them the wrong idea. Her hair was fastened back now, but on this blustery November day tendrils were escaping and the high-lighted streak was eye-catching.

When Paul Burnley had to turn to the little man who looked like an old jockey, who had climbed out of the van behind her, he seemed to be finding it hard to keep his eyes off Clare Rickard.

For Clarry the house was as magical inside as out, as if time had stood still since the name was changed from The Hall to King's Lodge, because Charles Stuart had found refuge here after the bloody battle of Worcester.

He had slept, with a price on his head, in the four-poster bed in the King's Room, hiding in the priest's hole from the searching Roundheads. And after three days he had been smuggled out in the night to the next Royalist house on the escape route to France and the years in exile before his return as Charles the King.

The fireplace in the King's Room was top of the list, and in the agent's office they worked out an agenda and agreed on terms, and everything seemed almost too good to be true.

The bedroom Clarry was given on the top floor was like something out of a period film, with its dark cream plastered walls crisscrossed with black beams. The bed was under the window, and she was pleased about that: she didn't sleep well in the dark.

She ran fingertips over a little oak table that gleamed like satin and smelled of lavender, and the wind in the chimney of a small cast-iron fireplace sighed softly.

It was a lovely little room, but she couldn't wait to wander around on her own and soak in the atmosphere of the old house. As soon as the girl who had shown her up here had gone she came downstairs again. She was going to the King's Room first, the heart of the house, where she would be starting on the carved stone fireplace in the morning.

She met no one on her way down from the attics or walking along the corridors, and she slipped quietly into the empty room, looking around again at the dark oil paintings, the furniture, the massive bed.

A faded brocade cover matched curtains looped around and the pelmet above, and impulsively she kicked off her shoes, swung her legs up and lay down, closing her eyes and staying very still.

If Charles Stuart had slept in here it must have been from utter exhaustion, because he surely had had enough on his mind to keep him from sleep for ever. If he did sleep she hoped his dreams were of a golden future, and not the nightmare of civil war and the shadow of the headsman's axe.

She could still hear the wind in the chimneys, and imagine a footfall, a movement, someone coming closer, until she opened her eyes and saw a man at the foot of the bed and a face from her own nightmares.

She shot up convulsively and rolled to the edge, nearly falling off, her feet scrabbling frantically for her shoes. He was so *big*, and thick dark brows, a thatch of dark hair and a slightly battered nose gave him the look of a bruiser. She had known he was a powerful man, but his physical presence was overwhelming.

'I'm starting on the fireplace in the morning,' she babbled.

'You get a good view of it from the bed.' Not lying there with her eyes closed, she wouldn't, and the deep drawling voice seemed familiar too, although she had never spoken to him before.

'Sorry.' She hated apologising, but of course she shouldn't be lolling on priceless antiques.

'Not many can resist trying the King's bed for size.'

Her lips wouldn't curve so she couldn't even pretend to smile back. 'Even you?' she heard herself ask.

'Every night.' With an ego like his it was a sure thing he would take over the King's Room, and she had to get out or she would never stop shaking.

'See you,' she said inanely, and sidled from the room, almost running until she had turned a corner. Nobody was following. She could hear a clock ticking somewhere but no footsteps and no voices, and she leaned against the wall, her folded arms gripping so tightly that her fingers dug through the thick sweater into the soft flesh of her upper arm.

Nicolas Dargan had given her the fright of her life. Anybody looming up like that would have startled her, but she was astonished at the violence of her reaction when she had opened her eyes and seen him looking down at her.

Her heart was still hammering wildly, and it would not have taken much to have had her running again, right out of King's Lodge. She might still do that. It was an option if she couldn't pull herself together.

The estate manager was still in his office on the ground floor, where they had discussed a contract that had been too good to be true if it meant working in Nicolas Dargan's bedroom.

'I've just met Nicolas Dargan,' Clarry said. Cole to his friends—she was never of their number.

'Good.' Then he saw her expression. 'No?'

'You said he wasn't staying here.'

'I said you'd be dealing with me, but it is his house. It's almost his village.' A job lot with King's Lodge thrown in, that didn't surprise her. 'Why?' he was asking. 'Is there a problem?' and she countered his question with another.

'Do you get much trouble with him?'

'There's been no trouble here. I've managed the estate for the last five years, I was taken over with it, and Dargan Enterprises have been the saving of us. But the boss does have a name for sailing near the wind.' He sounded as if that was something to admire. 'A bit of a buccaneer—have you come up against him before?'

She made herself smile. 'Oh, I've heard things. I just feel he could be dangerous, so I shall keep out of his way.' He smiled with her, and she said, 'See you later,' and stopped smiling as soon as she was out of the room.

She had hoped he would tell her that Nicolas Dargan would be gone tomorrow, but he didn't know, and it was stupid to feel trapped. It was a small world and Dargan Enterprises covered a wide area, and this was just coincidence, but the lovely old house had lost some of its charm, and she wondered if Charles Stuart had been glad to escape from here.

In the room under the eaves again she sat on her bed, slim jean-clad legs crossed, fingers laced over a kneecap, reliving what had happened to her that morning when she and Nigel Dargan had gone riding together.

The Dargans were cousins. There was no one else, that was the family. Nicolas owned everything, but Nigel worked for the company, and Nigel had wanted to marry her.

Clarry remembered how happy they had been. The sun had been shining and the cherry trees were a foam of pink blossom, but the blossom was long gone before she saw the trees again. Now she pushed back her hair, and beneath the white streak above her right temple was the familiar ridge of scar.

She couldn't recall the horse bolting and throwing her, nor the lost weeks of her life when she lay in a coma, but she would always remember that when she regained consciousness Nigel had been transferred to their office in Brussels. Nicolas had seen to that. Nicolas always made the rules. When he told Nigel, 'Start living your own life,' that was what had happened.

There was even another girl. Nicolas's choice again, but Clarry could imagine the pressure that had been put on Nigel. Nobody had held out much hope in the early days that she would not be brain-damaged, and seeing someone he cared for like that for weeks on end must have been hell for a sensitive man.

Nigel had suffered, she knew, but there had been no pity from Nicolas. He had consulted the medical reports and decided that a Dargan's best interests did not lie with a girl who could be a permanent liability. Nigel was given no choice, he was shipped out and kept away, and now she had seen and spoken to Nicolas in the flesh. Briefly, but it was enough for her to recognise a brute force against which Nigel would never have stood a chance.

When she came out of the coma it seemed that she had lost everything: job gone, home gone; and when she asked for Nigel it was days before he came.

She was weak, a shadow, and while he stammered she knew that she had lost him too. But her mind had been clearing, strength would soon be flowing back into her, and a fierce determination to be independent in the future was the best of therapies.

She had never expected to see Nigel again, and God knew she had never wanted to meet Nicolas, but she had recognised him at once, although she had never met him before. He had turned up on TV and radio from time to time, being interviewed about this and that, and if she was alone she rushed to turn him off. If there was anyone with her she tried to shut the sight and the sound of him from her mind, but that had to be why he had seemed so terrifyingly familiar standing at the foot of her bed.

Of course he wouldn't recognise her, and she doubted if he had ever given the girl his cousin had once loved a second thought, once that little matter was satisfactorily settled. She was a stranger to him, here to do the restoration work, and if she should come across him again she would act the stranger. Because she had this crazy conviction that she must keep her secret, that once she had been Nigel's Clarry. That if Nicolas Dargan found her out something shattering might happen.

Just before seven she went down to the little parlour that would be their day-room while they were here. She was still wearing the casual clothes she had arrived in, but she had washed and applied fresh make-up and her hair fell loose, touching her shoulders.

Once her hair had reached her waist. Then it had been a close crop. Before that her head was shaved, although she had hardly been aware of that. But she had watched the growing into an urchin cut, a short uneven bob and a longer, and now it waved strong and shining, the white streak the only reminder of unflattering styles that had gone before.

The staircase linked three galleried landings. From any you could look down the stairwell to the quarry-tiled floor, and as Clarry walked down the plain wooden staircase from the attics a woman appeared on a lower landing.

Wall brackets threw a good light on her silver-gilt hair, and what looked like a soft grey fur coat but these days was probably a high-fashion fake. On the stairs she heard Clarry's footsteps above and paused to look up, staring hard and briefly, then continuing her descent well ahead.

Who was that? Clarry wondered, and decided it was probably Miss Stretton, the lady of the manor as was. In that coat she was clearly on her way out somewhere, and Clarry hoped Nicolas Dargan was too, because if she should find herself at the same table as him she would never manage to get the food down.

That worry came to nothing. A table was laid for three in the parlour, where Paul Burnley joined them. The estate was his pet subject, and how the recession had been draining them until Dargan Enterprises came to the rescue. He sounded, Clarry thought, like a schoolboy rooting for his football team, and she asked cynically, 'What are Nicolas Dargan's plans for this house? A conference centre, or an apartment block? And of course there'll be a helicopter pad where the bluebell wood used to be.'

'What bluebell wood?'

He smiled uncertainly at her, and she said gaily, 'I don't know. He just strikes me as the sort who'd tarmac over bluebell woods. I don't have much faith in rich men who are built like all-in wrestlers.'

Danny's leathery face was bland, and Paul Burnley said, 'As far as I know, the house is staying a private residence.'

'Do you live here?' Clarry asked.

'I've a flat over the stables.'

'Are you married?' She could not have cared less. Her aim was to stop him burbling on about Nicolas Dargan in that sickening fashion.

'No.' But he was flattered she'd asked and very ready to talk about himself. By the end of the meal they knew a lot about the estate manager, and most of it was rather boring.

When Danny said, 'Goodnight, all,' and took himself off to his room, Paul Burnley said,

'You haven't seen the gardens, have you? I usually take a walk round the grounds last thing,' and Clarry went with him to a back door to check on the night.

The moon was bright and the stars were out. The wind had dropped to a chilly little breeze, and she borrowed a jacket from a row of coats and waterproofs hanging on the wall.

She had a small torch in her shoulder-bag. She switched that on for the first few steps, but the moon gave enough light for a late-night stroll, mainly across lawns, but there was a rose garden, a kitchen garden, a small orchard and a maze.

Paul Burnley kept pointing out what he considered the high spots, although Clarry would have welcomed a little silence in which to enjoy the old gardens by moonlight. He was like a puppy dog, so eager to please that she was tempted to pat him on the head and say, 'Down, boy!'

He led her to the entrance to the maze with a beaming smile, and it was an unusual feature—a Jacobean folly that had survived. Dense yew hedges were cut back straight and high, and by daylight it would be fun to roam around trying to find your way out. At night the narrow entrance was less inviting when Clarry peered in, shining her torch to where a wall of yew blocked the passage and one was faced with one's first choice of left or right.

'Do you want to go in?' Paul asked.

'Just a little way, then,' and after a couple of turns they came to a stone bench. The paths were covered with soft moss, but somehow Clarry had managed to ship a small sharp stone into her shoe. She sat down and tipped it out and shivered, and said, 'Think we could go back now? It's not all that warm, is it?'

As they came out Paul Burnley said, 'If you're interested, there's a copy of the plan on the wall in my office.'

Old designs of any sort, from wallpapers to blueprints, intrigued Clarry. 'I'd like to see that,' she replied.

It seemed a fairly simple plan, in black lines on paper the colour of parchment in a narrow black frame. The entrance was opposite a shaded area representing the house, and Clarry trailed a finger on the glass the way they had gone, following the circuitous route to the centre and trying to memorise as she went. When Paul asked, 'Will you join me in a coffee?' she said,

'No, thank you. I've enjoyed today, but tomorrow will be busy, I must say goodnight now.'

She walked up the stairs, examining pictures and a blue and yellow glaze vase in a window alcove. There was a small bathroom next door to her bedroom, and she went in there first. She would return this jacket in the morning, and she was slipping it off when she missed her shoulder-bag. She had gone out with it, taking her torch out of it. The torch was in her jacket pocket now and she could have left the bag in the office.

She hadn't, though. What she had done was drop it on that seat when she sat down and took off her shoe. Then they had decided to turn back and she had walked away without it. It really didn't matter; she could collect it in the morning.

But it did have her cheque-book, her credit cards and her keys, and if it should 'walk' before she reached it that would be an awful nuisance. When she started thinking she knew she wouldn't rest unless she fetched it.

The seat was only a couple of turns into the maze and she had just finished memorising the plan. She had a torch, so if that bank of cloud should drift over the moon she would still be able to see her way.

She hurried back across the turf and into the entrance, going confidently, the beam of her torch throwing a steady light. Here she turned right, then a little further and left, and just along the path was the stone seat set into the high hedge where she had stopped to shake out the little stone.

Only there was no seat. She could hardly credit it, but she must have gone wrong somewhere. There could be a hidden alley that wasn't marked, or perhaps they had taken a turn she hadn't noticed coming in the first time. That stone in her shoe had been irritating her almost at once.

She began retracing her steps to start again, but lichen covered the paths like a carpet and the rigidly controlled hedges were all the same height, and when she came into what should have been the way to the entrance/exit but wasn't she stood there, shaking her head.

She had managed to get lost in a quarter acre of hedges, and she had to find her own way out, because nobody would be looking for her. She hadn't even found her bag, and she was facing the wrong direction now; the faint glow in the sky from the house was behind her.

The darn place seemed booby-trapped, but the way out faced the house, so she would make for that, and soon she had to come on the path that would open on to the lawns.

If she was not out in a few more minutes she would have to shout for help. Someone would hear her. The maze was near the house and the wind was only a murmur now. But a right idiot she would look calling up a rescue operation at this time of night, and she decided to keep moving.

In the meantime her torch threw a comforting little searchlight, and although she was not enjoying herself much this was going to make Danny smile when she told him about it in the morning. She was in no way worried. Until she heard Nicolas Dargan shout, 'Hello, there!'

Then her reaction was the same panic that had yanked her off his bed. Her thumb jerked on the torch, switching it off, and she found herself ducking and scuttling, trying to keep out of sight.

She hoped she was out of sight. Upstairs overlooked the maze, but in the dark it must be impossible to follow anyone unless they were showing a light. She had to get away before he came down, but why should he come down? Her torchlight had gone out guiltily as soon as he shouted, but what harm could a prowler do in a maze: vandalise the hedges?

She kept her torch off, and then she heard him call again, nearer this time, ground level. While she was creeping along she could see the light from his torch flashing down the avenues and she knew she should be answering, 'I'm here!' but she couldn't have croaked the words. And when his head suddenly appeared over the top of a hedge—he had to be standing on something, either that or he *was* eight foot high—she had to clamp her teeth on her bottom lip to stop herself shrieking with hysterical laughter.

'What are you doing?' he asked.

Good question! Clarry bit her lip hard and then she managed to say, 'Trying to find my bag—I left it in here a little while ago.'

'Stay where you are.' He couldn't know she had been dodging him, and now she had to stand and wait, although that crazy impulse to run was still almost irresistible.

He came out at the end of the pathway, a dark shadow behind the beam of his torch. The moss underfoot muffled sound, but she knew he would move as quietly as a panther, and she took a dragging step to meet him.

'What happened to your torch?' he asked.

'It went out.' If he took it and tried it he would know she had switched it off. She dropped it into her pocket and bluffed, 'It's been on the blink.'

'Where did you leave your bag?'

'On a seat near the entrance. I thought I could just pick it up, but it isn't that easy.'

'Down here.' She was glad he turned back to lead the way. The paths were narrow, he might have touched her in passing, and she shrank at the thought. As it was, his broad shoulders seemed to block out the way ahead when she followed him.

They reached a seat, and there was her bag, and they were on the lawn in no time at all. She said, 'Thank you. Goodnight.'

'Goodnight, Clarry.'

Only those who knew her well used her pet name. She was Clare to the rest. 'You know who I am?'

'Of course.'

This was the last thing she had wanted, and how had it happened? 'Is that why I've got this contract?' she demanded. 'Was giving me a break Nigel's idea?'

When he said no, she gasped.

'It couldn't be your conscience? You couldn't feel you owed me?'

'Owed you for what?'

'For moving Nigel out of my life. You did do that?'

'I did.'

'In his best interests, of course.'

She made that heavily sarcastic, and he drawled, 'Well, it doesn't seem to have done you much harm.'

Rage was blurring her sight and her speech. She said raggedly, 'It could have finished me for all you cared. But you have a reputation for cutting away the dead wood, don't you? And there was a time when that was all I was.'

He had treated her heartlessly when she had been helpless, and now he said, 'You look remarkably fit to me,' and she could have clawed his arrogant face.

She spoke through gritted teeth. 'Oh, I'm fighting fit. Don't worry, I've got steady hands again.' That would have been hard to prove. If she had held out her hands anger would have had them shaking. 'I'm not going to wreck your chimneypieces—I know how you feel about your property. Talking of your property, how is Nigel these days?'

'Very well.'

'Remember me to him. Tell him I think of him often.' That was not true. She did not often think of Nigel, but it seemed a sharp line to walk away on.

By the time she was climbing the final staircase she was furious with herself for losing her cool like that. It was bad luck that had kept her on a crashing collision course with Nicolas Dargan today, and that he knew she was the girl his cousin might have married if he had not ended everything between them.

But he was in no doubt now how hostile and embittered she was, because she had just gone out of her way to spell that out for him, saying more than enough to bring down his formidable clout on her own stupid head.

CHAPTER TWO

CLARRY crept into her bed by the window and sat hunched and tense in the moonlight. Somewhere she had once come across an old country saying that if moonlight fell on you while you slept it could steal your soul. She would rather have moonlight than darkness, but that meeting with Nicolas Dargan just now seemed to have sent her moon-mad.

Until today she had not realised how traumatically he could affect her. If it had been Nigel here at King's Lodge he would not have aroused anything like this storm of emotion.

She had loved Nigel, they had had good times together, and if their paths crossed again she would feel a little sorrow, a little regret. But that would be all. Nigel might cast a shadow over her day, but coming face to face with Nicolas Dargan had hit her like a hurricane.

Heaven knew what tomorrow would bring. Whether she could work here. Whether she would get the chance, because Nicolas Dargan would hardly be wanting somebody around who had just told him they hated his guts.

She would have to wait and see, there was nothing else she could do. A headache was beginning to throb in her temples, but even if she did manage to sleep Nicolas Dargan would haunt her nightmares.

She woke next morning without being able to remember if she had dreamt but with him already on her mind so vividly that she blinked as she opened her eyes, expecting to see him at the side of her bed looking down at her.

Downstairs in the little parlour Danny was tucking into breakfast with a good appetite. Clarry needed coffee, but she found even a slice of toast hard to swallow.

Yesterday Paul Burnley had shown them an old mirror in a wide frame of elaborately carved oak. The design was fruit and flowers and the workmanship was superb, but over the years the frame had been damaged badly in one place where a corner was broken off.

Clarry had said they could repair it, and Danny had nodded sagely, because he was as skilled a woodcarver as the old masters, and she knew without him saying a word how much he wanted to carve a rose that would never die among the creations of craftsmen who had lived long ago.

This morning she would have to tell him he might not get the chance, but while she was taking a deep breath to start, 'Look, I'm sorry, but——' Paul Burnley walked in, bright and breezy.

'Morning, everybody. Everybody sleep well? Message for you.' For Clarry. 'Nicolas Dargan wants to see you.' He was overdoing the breeziness, she thought. 'Ten o'clock, if that's convenient.'

She would have liked to say, 'It isn't,' but she knew that was a bogus civility. Ten o'clock, Nicolas Dargan had said, and ten o'clock she had better be there. Wherever. 'Where?' she asked.

'There's an office leading off the King's Room.' She hadn't noticed, but the panelled walls could conceal doors.

Danny had finished breakfast, and now he said, 'Wait, shall I?' but Clarry wanted him gone. She couldn't forewarn him with the estate manager here, and she could well need time to get over what might be going to happen. Danny waiting for her when she came out of that interview could reduce her to the screaming abdabs.

She said, 'No need. It doesn't really need both of us. You know what we'd be bringing back for work and I've got a bag packed in my room, if you'd pick that up for me.'

Danny nodded and went, and she waved goodbye-for-now to the van with Paul Burnley standing beside her and asked him, 'How did my name come up for this? We're not that well known yet.'

'You were recommended to me. You did some work on a house in Stratford.'

So that was how it had happened, and she should be ringing and thanking the Mountjoys, because they had thought they were doing her a favour, putting prestigious and profitable work her way. It was not their fault their recommendation had brought her up against the man she would have paid good money to avoid.

Walking back to the house she asked, 'Have you seen Nicolas Dargan this morning?'

'No. There was a note on my desk.'

'So you've no idea why he wants to see me?'

She had wondered if the agent might have been told there were doubts about the restoration team, but he said, 'No, I haven't, but he's employing you and he likes to run a happy ship.'

Clarry's grin was a grimace. 'A buccaneer running a happy ship! Why don't you fly the Jolly Roger?' When Paul Burnley looked blank she explained, 'The pirates' skull and crossbones flag,' and he was suddenly on his dignity.

'I know what the Jolly Roger was, and Nicolas Dargan is tough. But he's a sound man, he looks after his own.'

That he did. He had done his ruthless best for Nigel when Clarry was dumped as damaged goods.

'But I'm not one of his own,' she said. 'He can send me packing if my face doesn't fit,' and she was rather touched when Paul Burnley tried to reassure her that he could not imagine anyone not being charmed by her face.

She left him at the door of his office and went upstairs to collect the small camera that would have been the first tool she used if everything had gone according to plan. Then back into the parlour, where the coffee-pot yielded a final cup. Sitting quietly now, she decided that she *did* want this contract. If she kept calm and businesslike this morning Nicolas Dargan might let the arrangements stand. He might even agree that the Dargans owed her some small compensation.

Just before ten o'clock she reached the door of the King's Room. It was open, and through another door she glimpsed another room. But then she saw Nicolas Dargan and everything else went slightly out of focus.

He was by the fireplace, wearing dark grey trousers and grey rollneck sweater. Just standing, waiting, but when she met his eyes she couldn't turn her head away. 'Good morning,' he said, and her answering good morning was a mumble.

'About this work you're doing for me—do I have your assurance you won't undermine the foundations?'

He had to be laughing at her, and she thought, it would be a red letter day for me if I could undermine you. 'I wouldn't know how,' she said, 'I'm not into demolition.'

He did laugh. Then he asked, 'How large is your staff?'

He couldn't know much about her or he would have known that. She said, 'There's just the two of us. I hope to take on an apprentice before long, but for now it's Daniel Hill. He's very experienced, he does wonderful work. He'd retired, but when I started up on my own he joined me.'

'He came out of retirement? How old is he?'

He didn't seem impressed, and she said defensively, 'What's his age matter? He's exceptional, and his work's as good as ever.'

'I'd like to meet him.' Danny wouldn't appreciate being grilled by Nicolas Dargan.

'You can't right now,' she said. 'He's gone to fetch what we'll be needing, he'll be back this afternoon. Your agent took us round yesterday and showed us what you wanted done. We can handle it.'

After she had been so hostile last night he was bound to have qualms about her and, ironically, if he watched her at work he would make her so jittery she could be making mistakes. 'Are you staying here?' she asked.

'Yes.'

'You're going to live in the house?'

'That's why I bought it,' he explained.

'Came as a job lot, did it, with the village?'

'No,' he said. 'What are you starting on?'

'What?' That sounded as though the contract was still on. Nothing had been signed yet, but he had not thrown them out. 'Oh, I should be doing this chimneypiece.' She held up the little camera she had been clutching, trying to sound the expert she was. 'But first we take photographs so that we have before-and-after records. Particularly where repairs as well as cleaning might be needed.'

This fireplace had signs of neglect. She had been standing just inside the door, but now she stepped forward. 'If you wouldn't mind moving.' Because he had not moved and he did obstruct quite an area.

'Don't say it,' he said.

She raised eyebrows. 'Say what?'

'That I could do with a repair job.'

It was the last thing she was likely to say, and she surprised herself when she asked, 'With all your money, why don't you get your nose fixed?'

'It's hardly worth it. It's been like this for a long time.'

'How did it happen?' She felt that Nigel had told her, but she couldn't quite remember.

'I got into a fight. When I was younger and a long way from home.'

'You lost?' She hoped so, but she couldn't imagine Nicolas Dargan on the losing side. He was a tough man in every way, hard muscles and a mind like a steel trap.

'It evened out, and by the time this had settled down I'd got used to it. I've always looked like a heavyweight contender. This could be the nose I should have been born with.'

There seemed hardly any family resemblance between the Dargan men. Nigel had a straight nose and a sensitive mouth. Nicolas's mouth was sensual and Clarry would have described it as cruel. His eyes were much darker, and so piercing that it was all she could do to meet them with a level stare.

'That streak in your hair,' he said, and she put a hand to touch it, or hide it, and started to say,

'Highlights are fashionable.' Then she said, 'It was the accident. It grew back this way.'

'So we've got something in common,' he remarked.

'Like what?' she said derisively.

'We're both flawed.'

She had to laugh at that. 'But mine's a very small flaw, I could put mine right myself with a home dye. Yours needs structural attention.'

The young woman walked in while they were laughing. Her smile was brilliant, and a little strained as if it had just been switched on. She kept looking at Nicolas Dargan and went straight to him as though there was no one else in the room.

'This is Clare Rickard,' he said.

'I'm here to do the cleaning and restoration,' explained Clarry.

'And this is Fiona Stretton,' said Nicolas.

She had smooth pale blonde hair and she was wearing a beige suede trouser suit and a cream silk shirt. Her skin was velvety, her eyes were pale blue, and she was still smiling, showing small even teeth. 'I saw you on the stairs,' she said. 'You seem to be making yourself at home.'

'Clare and I are old friends,' said Nicolas, and she gave Clarry a chilly sidewards glance.

'How convenient,' she said coolly. Then her voice warmed as she turned back to the man. 'I came to remind you about lunch. At the golf club.'

'No, thank you.'

'But my friends are expecting you.'

'Another time.'

'But——' Whatever her argument was going to be she gave in without voicing it. 'You're busy,' she said sweetly. 'I understand.'

Very undemanding, thought Clarry, standing back. Although I would put Fiona Stretton down as a girl who'd always demanded the best and got it.

Fiona went, still smiling for Nicolas, and Clarry said, 'We are not old friends.'

He shrugged broad shoulders, but he knew that. They had once had a mutual friend, which was a very different matter, and now she said with faint mockery, 'Or is that how you describe all your employees? Paul Burnley says you like to run a happy ship.'

'Does he, now?'

He must know he had a fan in the estate manager, just as anyone could see that Fiona Stretton was setting her cap at him. Clarry had no patience with the attitude of either, but Paul Burnley was likeable, while it would be easy to dislike Fiona. She said, 'If you did get mutiny aboard I should expect you to make them walk the plank rather than bother about keeping them happy.'

'Are you going to mutiny?' he queried.

'Why should I?' All she wanted was the chance to do her work, as well and as fast as possible. 'I'll be happy enough,' she said, 'if you let me get on and keep out of my way.'

'I don't keep out of anyone's way.'

He was still smiling, but it was a chilling reminder of how implacable he could be. She could imagine him towering over poor Nigel, not giving an inch, and she asked, 'What's the girl like that you picked for Nigel?'

She had gone too far again, but he spoke with what sounded like detached amusement. 'Let's get this straight. If you want to work for me, fair enough, but if you're staying we shall be seeing a lot of each other, it isn't that big a house, and I'm not employing you as a sparring partner, it would be too uneven a contest.'

'Wouldn't it, though,' she muttered.

'Unless you play a dirty game.'

'I don't.'

'Very high-minded, but it could put you at a disadvantage. Do you want the job?'

Clarry gulped, then admitted, 'Yes, I do.'

'Then we'd better call a truce, or the next time you get lost in a maze after dark you could meet more than you bargained for.'

That couldn't be a real threat, he had to be taking this lightly, and she started to say, 'Or the next time I——' and held that back, because 'put my feet up on your bed,' was far too suggestive.

'So it's a truce?' Nicolas said, and when he held out a hand she had to take it.

But as their hands locked her breath caught, and her heart missed a beat, then pounded on furiously. His hand was cool and the pressure was light, but his touch seemed to reach the deepest nerves in her, so that if she had left her hand in his she could have been invaded body and mind.

It must have been brief, that handshake, for almost at once she was clutching her camera again. It was a wonder she hadn't dropped it. He had moved away from the fireplace and she went closer and pretended to peer at it, because the handshake had been a shaker. She had been kissed on the lips and felt far less, and she couldn't explain now what she had felt, almost a bonding, as if there was a living link between them.

That was not so. There was no bond between her and Nicolas Dargan. He was her old enemy, but if she wanted the contract she had to keep a civil tongue in her head while she was here. If she couldn't manage that it would not be for want of trying, and she began to take her photographs, concentrating harder than she needed on a simple routine task so that she felt rather than saw him go into the office through the door in the panelling.

When she stopped snapping he called, 'Hold on!'

She would have gone, but now she looked at the oil paintings again. They were all old scenes of the house and what she supposed was the local countryside, and as he came back she asked, 'Have they always been here?'

'They've mostly been bought with the Lodge. So has some of the furniture. This was the bed Charles slept in.'

If the Strettons had lived here for the last fifty years that meant it had been Fiona's home all her life. 'It must be hard to leave a place like this,' Clarry mused, and was almost sorry for Fiona, who had temporary rooms in her old home and designs on the man who was master here now.

An affair with Nicolas Dargan and she could keep her apartment, marry him, and King's Lodge was hers again. Marriage might be harder to manage. Clarry remembered Nigel saying Cole was not the marrying sort... 'He gets some gorgeous girls, but he never buys a wedding ring...'

Of course, he could have changed his ideas since then. Fiona Stretton could be the ideal partner here, and she was already playing her part. Nicolas Dargan did not tolerate dissent, so she was sweet-talking him. They could suit each other. He was a cold-blooded character, and to Clarry Fiona had seemed to have more than a touch of ice maiden.

She looked at Nicolas, and the crazy notion that he knew what she was thinking seized her so that she could feel herself starting to blush. She turned her head quickly, the fall of her hair swishing across her burning cheek, looking at the nearest painting and saying the first thing that came into her mind. 'They're scenes from round here, aren't they? Do you know where this was?'

The foreground was a wide rough track. Behind were low hills, a cluster of cottages and a church steeple. 'It's the old road.' Nicolas crossed to the window. 'Seen from here.' She went to stand beside him and look down. Behind the creeper-covered walls and the gates was a narrow lane. On the skyline traffic was moving along a busy highway.

'The main road ran just in front of the house until about a hundred years ago,' he told her. 'Charles stood at this window and watched men who had fought for him trudging back to Scotland.'

Some would be wounded, all would be weary and defeated, hungry and thirsty. Clarry could imagine the day would be grey like today, and a flurry of leaves blown in the wind went like a ragged garment. 'How could he bear it?' she wondered aloud. 'Didn't he want to go out and give them food, something?' and she knew how stupidly impulsive she was sounding, she didn't need him to explain.

'There'd have been a high price to pay,' he said. 'Once it was known they were hiding Charles Stuart every man and woman in the house would have been strung up.'

'All the same it must have been dreadful. And terrifying.'

'I agree. But don't shiver for them.'

A little tremor was running down her spine. Not exactly a shiver, more like a finger touch trailing on bare skin from the nape of her neck. It could have been her imagination reliving the terrifying past, or it could be because Nicolas Dargan was so close. 'They got him away,' he said. 'The operation was a success.'

'Dargan Enterprises couldn't have handled it better?' she said lightly.

'I don't think they could.'

'Is that why you wanted the house, for a tourist attraction?'

'I see no reason why the public shouldn't be admitted, it's everyone's heritage, but I've bought the Lodge to live here. We've got land and property in the area. I heard the house was for sale and I came to see it.'

Clarry wondered if his first sight of the house was his first meeting with Fiona, or did they know each other before and was it Fiona's suggestion that had brought him here? None of which was any of Clarry's business.

'When I turned in through the gates,' he said, 'I knew that if anyone was buying this house it was going to be me.'

She gave a mock sigh. 'How fabulous to be rich! When I drove my little van in I thought, how lovely, and how rotten that I can't have it.'

Suddenly she was fooling with him, and when he asked, 'So what are you going to do for us?' she was eager to explain, as if it was giving her a small share in the house.

'This chimneypiece, cleaning and there's some cracking, that's all in this room.'

'Show me the rest.'

On this floor several rooms needed attention, where panelling veneer had split, marquetry had lifted and lacquer flaked. Fireplaces needed cleaning. There was furniture with a build-up of wax polish to be removed, a table on rickety legs.

She had the list in her mind and she went round, pointing out the items. When they came to the mirror with its carved frame she said, 'Danny wants to do this.'

The antique glass had clouded so that reflections were misty and the white streak in her hair was dull silver. Nicolas Dargan, a man in grey, loomed beside her, his head brushing the low-beamed ceiling. He was looking down at her, not at their image. 'He's a wood carver?' he queried.

'The best,' she said. 'He used to make the most incredible toys—I've still got some of them. A griffin he carved for my fourteenth birthday—you should see that!'

'You seem very fond of him.'

'We're not really related, but he's always been a kind of grandfather to me. He was my grandfather's friend, they worked together.' When she paused Nicolas waited and everything was quiet. 'Am I talking too much?'

'No,' he said, and she went on.

'My grandfather died before I was born and I lost my parents in my teens, but Danny was always there. The work I do, I suppose I inherited the knack from my grandfather, and I was trained, but Danny taught me so much.' She hesitated again. 'Why do you want to know?'

'You interest me,' he explained.

'Why?'

'Because you're here, and the odds against that have got to be considerable.' His expression told her nothing except that he was watching her. 'Burnley had a free hand, he was told to get anything repaired that needed repairing, and he comes up with Rickard Restoration.'

'How did you know that was me?' Clarry asked.

'There was publicity a year ago when you started up.'

So there was. Even the nationals had given a picture and a write-up to the Sleeping Beauty who had recovered so well she was launching her own small firm. For a little while everyone knew what kind of business Clare Rickard was in.

'I've only had local publicity since,' she said, 'but we're doing quite well.'

'Good.'

'We are good,' she assured him.

'Then I can probably put more work your way.'

Work would be welcome, but she didn't want him patronising her, and she said, 'I don't want any favours.'

'While you're getting that white streak removed,' he said, 'you might do something about the chip on your shoulder.'

Her lips parted to say, That's no chip, that's the weight of past experience; but before she could speak he said, 'Remember the truce,' and his smile was something.

Clarry had never thought of him smiling. He had always been the tycoon, with all Nigel's prospects in his pocket. Nigel had always spoken of his cousin as a grim and dominating figure, and the image in her mind was never of Cole Dargan smiling.

Now she knew that when he did smile, the way he was smiling at her, his smile could warm a dark-panelled room.

'Of course I remember the truce,' she said gaily. 'I better had, hadn't I, or I'm off the happy ship. Well, it's the mirror frame in here and this fireplace, which has a fairly modern surround, more's the pity.'

He could see that, he knew that. She sounded like a teacher, and she grinned. 'This is ridiculous, me, showing you round your house.'

'But instructive—you're showing me faults I didn't know existed. Although perhaps I should be showing you around.'

Paul Burnley had taken them where they would be working. Walking the rooms with Nicolas Dargan would be quite different, and she said, 'I'd like that.'

'Good,' he said. 'Come on, Clarry.'

Something faint and faraway echoed in her mind like a warning bell, making no sense at all. He was going to show her round his home, for goodness' sake, not pull her off a cliff! She said, 'It's a fantastic house.'

'I think so,' he agreed.

For a while she put herself out to be knowledgeable and intelligent, to show him that if Nigel had waited for her he would not have made too bad a bargain. But when she relaxed Nicolas Dargan was an ideal companion.

He knew it all, of course. He answered her questions, he told her things, he would have made a cracking good tourist guide. And sometimes, as they walked through the quiet rooms and along the uneven floors of the narrow corridors, there were silences when she felt no need to search for something to say. That was pleasant. Usually you only got that kind of easiness with friends.

Of course she was always conscious of him. She had been wrong, thinking that everything was investment to him. He did value beautiful things for their own sake. When he picked up a brown-glazed stirrup cup, shaped like a sleek head of a hound, and held it in strong sensual hands, she could feel the caress on her own arm in little electric shocks, because Nicolas Dargan was a sexy man.

Nigel had told her about the women, but she had put most of Nicolas's success down to him being wealthy. That wouldn't hurt. Big money was a turn-on. But right now she would assess the cash as a bonus, because he had enough innate sensuality to weaken any red-blooded woman.

Not that she was weakening, but keeping the truce was getting less of an effort all the time. They went over most of the house. Three closed doors on the first floor were where the Strettons were staying. For the time being, Nicolas told her, and she wondered what he would say if she said, 'I shouldn't bank on their leaving.' But he must know what Fiona was about, and Clarry reminded herself again that it was no concern of hers.

In the dining-room one of the dailies was giving a final shine to the oak refectory table. Her name was Dolly. She was plump and middle-aged, and she smiled when they walked in and said, 'Morning, miss,' to Clarry, then entered into an animated conversation with Nicolas about her youngest, our Ivan, who had broken his leg on a school skiing trip last month.

Nicolas Dargan knew all about that. He seemed genuinely concerned, and amused to hear that Ivan's crutch had brought down a supermarket display of baked beans yesterday while he remained upright and unscathed.

Dolly seemed contented, polishing his table and telling him about her family. 'A happy ship,' said Clarry, when Dolly had left them. 'So long as they remember who the captain is.'

'Would you prefer the ship to sink?' queried Nicolas.

'Of course not.' That was the chip on her shoulder again, but she could understand why the villagers wanted him here, shouldering their burdens, and she was prepared now to be working for him herself. 'Honest,' she said, 'the thought of mutiny never crossed my mind.'

'Smart girl,' and she pretended to wince.

'I always stiffen when anyone calls me girl.' He raised a quizzical eyebrow and she went on, 'And it's nothing to do with Women's Lib. It's what Danny calls me when he thinks I'm making a fool of myself. He's a man of few words, is Danny, but if he says "Not on, girl," that means he has some very good reasons against whatever it is, and you'd better believe it.'

'I'll try to remember.'

'Thank you.' She was joking, but he didn't smile.

'It won't be hard,' he said, 'when you're so entirely a woman.'

Shock-waves surged through her, all her female hormones responding to his overwhelming male force, so that it would not have been hard to go to him like a mote of metal to a magnet. She had too much sense to do that, but holding back was leaving her blood tingling.

Having him around could sharpen your senses, she thought. All those virility vibes, even in small doses, would be a marvellous tonic. So long as she did keep her head, because, as she knew to her cost, Nicolas Dargan was a hell of a man.

He was not making a pass. He didn't follow that up in any way. They were by a window that overlooked the maze, and he looked down now and said, 'That was overgrown when I came, I had it tidied up.'

'And a super job they made. I've never seen a tidier maze.' Clarry smiled, and this time he smiled back. 'I looked at the plan of it last night,' she said, 'and I was sure I'd memorised it, but when I got inside I was hopelessly lost. That map in the office is right?'

'It's the original. The design was never changed.'

'Maybe it moves by moonlight.'

He chuckled. 'Not on, girl,' and she shook her head.

'That doesn't sound like Danny.' Danny was hollow-chested and croaky. Nicolas Dargan's voice had a deeper timbre entirely. 'Mind you, that's what Danny would have said. I hope——' She hesitated. 'I hope you'll like Danny. He can be an awkward old cuss.'

'We'll get along.' He sounded confident, but Danny knew what Nicolas had done, and it took a lot to change Danny's mind. Clarry hoped he would remember the rose and not be too stubborn.

If she saw him before Nicolas did she would tell him that having spent a while with Nicolas Dargan she had decided he was no money-grubber. He had bought this house because he wanted to live here, and he would be a caring custodian. She would not, of course, mention that in bed tonight, before falling asleep, she might possibly fantasise about making love with Nicolas Dargan.

That was all it would be, fantasy. It was unlikely he was going to proposition her, and if he should she would decline very firmly. She would never risk getting involved with this man. He was ruthless and he was dangerous, but he was the stuff erotic dreams were made of, and Clarry had a lively imagination.

Downstairs in his office the estate manager jumped up as they walked in. Clare Rickard seemed to have some sort of grudge against Nicolas Dargan, who had said he wanted to see her this morning. Since then Paul Burnley had been wondering what the outcome of that would be.

The next few minutes puzzled him. He had some papers for Nicolas Dargan, who read them, deleted and initialled, while Clare stood, arms folded, looking through the window. When he put the papers aside Nicolas went across to her and said, 'Shouldn't you be taking another look at this map?'

She laughed. 'I don't need to, I could draw it for you.' As she looked up at him he tucked a lock of hair behind her ear and she said, 'I've got a very good memory for patterns.'

'Except by moonlight.'

'When things tend to shift. In daylight I could take you straight to the centre.'

'You're on,' he said.

Calling goodbye as she went, with Nicolas Dargan's guiding hand on her arm, Clarry looked back at Paul Burnley. His face was blank and bewildered, as though he couldn't believe his eyes.

CHAPTER THREE

THE maze did look different by daylight. Clarry took the two turns that should have brought her to the seat and her left-behind bag last night, and this time the seat was where she expected it to be. 'I still can't see where I went wrong,' she said.

'You must have missed a turn in the darkness,' said Nicolas.

'I must have done.'

It was a fact that she had an almost photographic recall, and she stood for a moment now, eyes closed, 'seeing' that map on the wall again. Then she set off with the man following.

She was almost sure, except for a few times when she stopped to consider and got silent hints from his expression, turning it into a game that had her laughing most of the time. When that last little passage opened on a small lawn of moss and another seat she had done it—followed the path in her mind and reached the goal.

'How does it feel to get there?'

He was smiling at her, and she said, 'You should know. You usually do, don't you, and we're not talking mazes.' Then she gave a 'Tra-la!' of triumph and a quick twirl. She was pleased with herself. That had been fun.

The seat was set against the hedge too. It had a back and arms, and that was the only difference from the other two seats in the maze. She sat down and said, 'There should be something more.'

'Perhaps there was once, but there's no record of it. Or the seat might be enough depending on who was waiting here.'

There she sat, as if she was waiting, and she joked back, 'Or who you were sharing it with.'

'Exactly.' He sat down beside her, and it was like being in a little room: green walls, green carpet, overhead a metal-grey ceiling of sky. Restful, relaxing. Clarry let the peace flow over her and wondered if he would speak first and shatter the spell. She didn't think she would. She was content to sit here, with his arm along the back of the seat behind her, although only her hair was touching him.

The moss carpet was thick and soft underfoot and there was something dreamlike about this little green room, with a blackbird flying across up there. Another bird followed, and she watched their flight so that her head went back into the crook of Nicolas's arm.

If she had shot up it would have been making too much of a casual contact, and it was pleasant, her head cradled just right. A few more seconds, she thought, and I'll move. She kept her eyes half closed—lolling like this made you drowsy—and squinted up through extravagantly long lashes.

She knew what Nicolas looked like, she knew his face well, and the faint smell of aftershave was familiar. Someone else had used it, possibly Nigel. Four seconds more, five seconds she let her head rest, then she said, 'The question now is, can I find the way out again?'

'You got us in, I can always get us out,' and she grinned.

'That sounds like the offer I've been waiting for!' She got up reluctantly. 'First right?'

'Right,' he said, and they came out without stopping anywhere. Clarry was not certain whether she was finding the way or just taking the turns he was indicating, but when they came out she thought, I'm sure I could do it on my own. But she was not sure she would want to.

'It's about time for lunch,' he said, and she quipped,

'The clubhouse?'

'Very overrated.' She was getting away with some barefaced cheek. 'They do a reasonable meal here,' he said.

'So I hear.'

'Will you join me?'

'I'd like that. Your room or mine?'

They were all his rooms, and he said, 'The dining-room.'

'Lovely—I've taken a shine to that table.'

'Five minutes,' he said, and she went into the little cloakroom on the ground floor to wash her hands.

She was enjoying herself immensely, getting along with Nicolas Dargan so well that it was no longer surprising her. She got along with most folk. If her accident had never happened and she had been introduced to him as the girl Nigel wanted she felt he might not have stood in their way. Then she and Nigel could have stayed together. Married. That was what she had wanted then, but she had different aims now. Love left you open to hurt, and she liked her life safe, just the way it was.

She dried her hands and ran her fingers through her hair. Maybe she had left that white streak to remind herself what it was like being abandoned, and that none of her recovery had come from a lover's support.

Her white streak was a warning against falling in love again, but Nicolas Dargan's flaw hadn't kept him out of fights. He was a born fighter, and it *was* the nose he should have been born with. Clarry wondered if there were any early photographs and thought she would quite like to see them. Then she went up to the first floor and the dining-room. She had had hardly any breakfast and she was suddenly ravenously hungry.

He was there already. A girl who was laying the table for two set down a final fork and gave Clarry a very sharp look as they passed in the doorway. She was more used to seeing Fiona here, Clarry reckoned, and hoped Fiona would not decide to come home for lunch after all.

None of the rooms in the house was large. This table could have seated eight, so dinner parties would be small intimate affairs, but it was a well preserved period piece, and the chairs, two carvers and six with twisted bobbin legs and leather backs and seats, were a matching set.

Clarry sat down to the right of the bigger carver chair and looked at the heavy silver cutlery and gleaming glassware and almost asked, 'Do you always dine like this, even midday?' But she didn't, because he probably did.

Nicolas poured her a little white wine and she sipped, and it was delicious, going down cool and awakening her taste buds. She was not asking what that was either, because she was sure it was out of her range and if he told her she would be none the wiser. But when they brought in the first course she had to say, 'That looks marvellous.'

In a flat terracotta oven dish fish steaks had been grilled golden and garnished with parsley. Hot sweetcorn topped with strips of red pepper made it colourful enough for a cookery illustration, and there were lemon wedges, side salads, tiny boiled buttered potatoes and mange-tout peas.

Clarry could feel her mouth watering as she took her helping. She was a seafood addict, and halibut was a big improvement on fish fingers. She savoured and swallowed, then wondered if she was looking greedy and started toying with her food and making table talk, asking him, 'What are Dargan Enterprises going to do around here?'

'Give local firms a shot in the arm.'

'What sort of shot?'

'Advice. Finance. One project is the Shire Horse Centre—a stud farm and an arena for horse shows. They'll be selling tackle, saddles, bridles. It was a dairy farm that was going bankrupt, and the family had this idea but not enough backing to make it viable. Paul Burnley is enthusiastic about that, he'd be delighted to tell you all about it.'

Nicolas couldn't have seen any evidence that his agent fancied her, but he seemed to know, and she said gravely with dancing eyes, 'He is very enthusiastic, isn't he?'

'Very,' and somehow she was talking about herself again. Just rambling on, about music, books, food—she was tucking into this. Work. She told him about her neighbours and friends in the units, what Rickard Restoration had done in the first twelve months, and she smiled as she said, 'This is the first time the firm's slept on the job. It will be lovely, living in this house for a little while.'

'Where do you live?' asked Nicolas.

'In Danny's bungalow, in Moreton-in-the-Marsh.'

He seemed to be considering that. Then he said, 'I wouldn't have expected your live-in man to be your grandfather.'

Clarry had just put down her wine glass; now she picked it up again and took a couple of sips, and for the first time her voice was as slow as his. She had been chattering away, but now she spoke very slowly and deliberately. 'I didn't have much luck with a man nearer my own age. One day I woke up to hear he'd taken off on an offer he couldn't refuse.'

Nigel had not been living with her, he had just been a welcome guest, but Nicolas knew what she meant. 'And since then?' he asked.

'Since then they say goodnight and go home. The bungalow only has two bedrooms, and Danny is old-fashioned. Of course, anyone with a house this size could easily accommodate a live-in lover.'

She stopped there, as though she was listening to the echoes of what she had just said, realising how it might sound and gulping, 'I'm not offering——'

'No need to stress that,' Nicolas said drily, and in fact she had been thinking of Fiona, which was almost more tactless. But so was his questioning.

She touched her glass. She was usually a good listener, but telling him everything had seemed so natural, and she asked, 'Do you do business lunches? Can you get anyone babbling their secrets?'

When he smiled at that she had to smile too, and from then on he kept up his end of the conversation. He told her more about the village, what the people round here wanted, and she never doubted that everything he was planning would be done. But he was funny too, he could tell a hilarious tale, and she laughed a lot. It was one of the most enjoyable meals she could remember.

Dessert was served: apple pie, cheeses, fruit, and they had finished with that and were drinking coffee when there was a tap on the door. Nicolas called, 'Come in,' and Danny stood there.

'They said you were here,' he said, frowning disapproval of the scene he was viewing.

When Nicolas said, 'Come and sit down,' he approached the table, but his expression didn't change. He sat in the small armchair, the other end of the table, facing Nicolas and still scowling.

The main dishes had been cleared, but this was obviously the end of a very civilised meal. There was still wine in the bottle, and when Nicolas offered Danny shook his head, and Clarry said brightly, 'I've been shown over the house and round the maze, I've had a fascinating time, everything is absolutely——' she paused for emphasis '—absolutely fine.'

Danny sat like something he might have carved himself, silent and separated from them by the empty chairs.

Now let's see you get round Danny, she thought, but she didn't get the chance, because Nicolas said, 'Mr Hill, I want your advice. There's a carved altar rail in the church that I'd like you to see.'

He stood up, and Danny did too, but reluctantly, as if he suffered from arthritis, which he did not.

'You will excuse us?' Nicolas said to Clarry.

'Case is outside your door,' said Danny, following Nicolas Dargan out of the room.

Clarry went up to put away her clothes in the cupboard and drawers, then went on with the film record she had started earlier. She was photographing the big fireplace in the entrance hall when Danny came back. He was alone, the hall was empty, and from inside the chimney alcove she called, 'Everything all right?'

He grunted and headed for the staircase, but this time a grunt was not enough, and she went after him, catching him before the first gallery. 'Danny, is everything all right? We need the work, and he says he can find us more.'

Danny's mouth went down at the corners, and she climbed the stairs beside him, keeping her voice urgent and low. 'I don't want any trouble. You don't have to like him to work for him.'

'Just remember that,' said Danny.

His room was under the eaves too, along the passage from hers. Clarry went up beside him, wondering if she should ask about the altar rail and deciding to leave that till later.

On the top floor she said, 'We'll start tomorrow. I've taken the pictures, I'll take the King's Room chimneypiece, and you could start designing the missing piece for the mirror frame.'

She wanted to appease him, but Danny saw right through her and went straight back to the real issue. 'He's a hard man.'

'I know that,' she said. 'Everybody knows that.'

They were at the door of her room when he launched into what for him was quite a speech. 'Then don't you get changing your mind about him, because his sort never change.' He stomped off down the corridor and Clarry went slowly downstairs again.

In the early days of her recovery Danny had borne the brunt of her obsession against Nicolas Dargan. He was not forgiving in a hurry, but while Danny was here Nicolas had a craftsman who was incapable of doing less than his best work. Daniel Hill might not join the crew of the happy ship, but he would more than work his passage.

Clarry took a final photograph of the big fireplace and was walking towards the parlour when Paul Burnley came into the hall. 'I was hoping to catch you,' he said. 'I want to talk to you.'

'Yes?'

'Not here.' There was no one around, but he dropped his voice to a whisper. 'In private.'

'Sounds interesting,' smiled Clarry.

He waited until they were in his office with the door closed, then he said, 'You might tell me I'm taking too much on myself, I wouldn't be saying anything, except——' He paused, looking hot and bothered, and Clarry prompted:

'Except what——?' She could think of nothing the estate manager could tell her that should have him hopping around like this. 'You're not going to warn me we won't be getting paid? Dargan Enterprises couldn't be on the skids?'

'Lord no!' he exclaimed. 'Nothing like that. No, this is a personal matter.'

Good, she thought, although personal problems she could do without. 'Whatever it is,' she begged, 'do get on with it.'

'In strict confidence, you promise me that?'

'As the confessional. Well?'

'You didn't know Nicolas Dargan before you came here?'

'We'd never met,' she said.

'You seem to be getting on very well together. You had lunch together.'

'So?'

'I have the greatest respect for him,' said Paul Burnley fervently. 'He's a giant of a man. But there's a reserve about him, if you know what I mean. Nobody takes liberties with him, nobody gets familiar.'

The very thought of that silenced him for a moment, and Clarry nodded, indicating that she believed this even if she had no idea where it was leading.

'With you this morning he seemed—almost matey, didn't he?'

'Almost matey? Well, I suppose you could say that,' she agreed.

'But he doesn't carry on like that. It wasn't——' again he stumbled over the words '—it wasn't natural for him, I couldn't understand it at all.'

Why should you bother about it? she wondered.

'He's a spellbinder,' said his agent, 'and he's a manipulator. If he wasn't he wouldn't be what he is and where he is. He uses opportunities, he uses people. And when I thought about that I thought, that's what he's doing here.'

'Using me?' Clarry said crisply, 'Do you mean seducing me?' and if possible he looked even more uncomfortable.

'I don't think I do, although I wouldn't know about that. But this is the situation you're in.' Now it was all coming in a rush, 'Miss Fiona—Fiona

Stretton—is still living here, and nobody round here believes she's ever going to leave King's Lodge if she can help it.'

'Who could blame her?' Clarry murmured.

'Yes, well,' he looked around the empty room as if spies might be lurking, 'she and Mr Dargan are—well——'

'Very good friends?' Clarry suggested. A more raunchy term she felt would shock him speechless, and he had started stammering again.

'It does look like that. Only we all know from the way she's carrying on that she'd like it to be official, but he doesn't seem the marrying kind. With you on the premises and him taking up with you she might get the message.'

'That he's a womaniser who doesn't want a wife?'

The thought of Clare Rickard repeating all this to Nicolas Dargan hit him, and he sat down suddenly, asking himself, 'Why am I telling you this?'

'Because you think I should know?'

'You're a very attractive girl,' he said hoarsely. 'Dargan could have fallen for you as soon as he saw you. Why not?' his grin was wan. 'I could, but I'm not him. He never loses control, and he always ends up with them dancing to his tune. I don't want you to. Not in a case like this.' He gestured helplessly. 'It's just struck me as a likely reason—you must think I'm a fool.'

'I think you're a knight in shining armour,' she said. He hardly knew her at all and he could be risking his job warning her against reading too much in Nicolas Dargan's attentions. 'You're not a fool,' she said. 'You're smart. I've met "Miss Fiona" and anyone could see what she was up to; and Nicolas Dargan hasn't fallen for me, so if he gives that impression it could be to show her she's never going to be a one-and-only.'

'You don't mind?' asked Paul.

She shrugged. 'Why should I? It's flattering to be told I'm attractive, but I'm not conceited enough to go after one his size.'

Paul roared with laughter and relief, and Clarry thought, It isn't that funny.

So Danny was right again... 'His sort never change.' What Nigel had said about Cole never buying a wedding ring still held.

'Poor old Fiona,' said Clarry, and Paul Burnley agreed,

'She's a poor little rich girl. The old man has always given her everything, and she can't believe there are some things she can't have. And some men.'

'What's she like, apart from born lucky?'

'A bit of a bitch,' he admitted, and Clarry grinned,

'Well, he can be a bastard, so they could make a matching pair.' She sat back now, still smiling. 'It might be a lark if he does think he's using me. Do you think I should play up to him?' and immediately Paul was anxious again.

'Oh, I wouldn't advise that.' Nor would I, she thought. 'Would you——?' He stopped to clear his throat. 'Would you have dinner with me tonight? There's a little place I know.'

'Thank you, but not tonight.' Lunch had been meal enough for today, and she had had more than enough of her new friends for now.

'Clare and I are old friends,' Nicolas had told Fiona, implying something that did not exist, using Clarry from the beginning to distance Fiona.

When she left the office she went into the cloakroom on the ground floor to splash her face with cold water. The white streak in her hair seemed to blaze and blur as she blinked water from her lashes.

She should not have needed the warning against a manipulating man; the white streak should have been warning enough. But now she knew the reason for that 'truce' every time she spoke to Nicolas Dargan, or smiled when she was near him, she would feel like a puppet on a string, dancing to his tune. The hell I will, she promised herself, the *hell* I will!

Of course Clarry had not mentioned Paul Burnley's warning to Danny last night, and by the light of a new day it might have seemed no big deal. If Nicolas Dargan had explained the situation to her she might have said something like, 'Pleased to be of service, Rickard Restoration aims to help.'

No, she might not. She was still doing a slow burn as she sat brushing her hair, so hard that it sprang up following the brush. How dared he try to use her in any way but her professional capacity? She would not put herself out by a hair's breadth to make life easier for Nicolas Dargan. He was the last man on earth she would be doing any favours.

She had had the full charm treatment yesterday, and she should have wondered why he was wasting so much of his precious time on her. Well, she had the explanation, and she went on brushing her hair furiously until she realised she was creating a wild halo. Then she put away the brush and smoothed her hair down with her hands.

In workman's dungarees she went down to breakfast. Danny was in the same uniform, although his overalls were shabbier and older, and after breakfast they parted, Danny back to the mirror frame, to inspect and sketch and maybe dream. And Clarry to the King's Room.

She knocked on the door. It was after nine o'clock and she would have expected Nicolas Dargan to be an early riser; but this was his bedroom—she couldn't be wandering in. If he was still occupying the King's Bed, should she curtsy and say, 'Excuse me, Your Majesty, but would you close the curtains, the workers are here'?

It was no joke. Pretending it was was a nervous reaction she had to control. She drew deep breaths and waited, and when no one answered she opened the door.

The coverlet over the bed was smooth, and a step into the room reassured her that the room was empty. She was glad of that; she certainly did not want Nicolas around.

Perhaps he had slept in another bed last night. Fiona's, perhaps. Although not if he was supposed to be taking up with his 'old friend Clare' again. More likely he was up and about his business. He could be in the office behind the heavy panelling.

Clarry knew where the door was, but there was no indication of it on this side. Originally it was probably a robing-room, or even the priest's hole, although it was on the large side for that. Those hiding places were designed to conceal usually one fugitive in the smallest possible space.

This room was a likely location. The walls, wood panelled from floor to ceiling, offered no clues, and she began running her fingertips round moulding edges because that was where pressure points might be.

Suddenly one panel moved, so easily that it seemed to swish back, a sliding door opening not on a priest's hole but a bathroom. And Nicolas Dargan, stark naked and dripping wet, stepping out of a shower.

Clarry's throat closed as if a hand had gripped it and her mouth fell open. She lurched back, landing sitting on the edge of the bed, not knowing where to look or what to say.

He took the two strides to the door, and she managed to croak, 'S-sorry, I was going to start work.'

'Don't let me stop you.' The door slid shut, and for the first time in her life she got the curious sensation of an all-over burning blush.

Some time, when she was a long way away from here, this would be something to laugh about, but right now she was scalded with embarrassment. She had seen naked men before, but now she was as confused as a gauche schoolgirl, and she got off the side of the bed and went to the window as if the wind that was stirring the trees could reach her.

Should she clear off for a while, give him time to get dressed? Although that was probably a dressing-room as well as a bathroom. He'd have a bathrobe at the very least, he'd be covered when he came out, and if it seemed she couldn't face him she was going to look such a ninny.

So, she had walked in, but he should have locked the door. He probably never bothered, he would hardly be expecting visitors, but that wasn't her fault.

'Sorry about that,' she would say, cool and casual, if only she could stop blushing to the roots of her hair. He wouldn't be embarrassed, she was sure. He probably swam in the nude, slept in the nude.

The big frame carried no spare weight over the muscles. He was in superb physical shape, and it was no surprise to her that he was at home in his skin. He had that kind of confidence. Nakedness would not make him vulnerable. In a well cut suit or the way she had just seen him he was still Nicolas Dargan, man of power and don't you forget it.

She went over to the fireplace, taking her tools out of her bag, and repeating in her mind like a mantra... It was nothing to fuss about, nothing at all. But when she heard the bathroom door slide open she practically stuck her head up the chimney.

'Early for Christmas,' he said.

'I'm looking for loose bricks,' she said, lying without a qualm. 'I hate things falling on me.'

'I know how you feel, I'm not fond of sudden shocks myself.' She had to straighten up and face him.

He was dressed formally, shirt, tie and jacket, and his dark hair was thick and strong enough to have shaken off the shower. 'Did you want the bathroom, or were you checking the panelling?' he asked, and she stuttered.

'I didn't know—there was a bathroom, I thought there might be a priest's hole. There is, isn't there? Charles hid in it, didn't he?'

'Not down here. On the top floor.'

'Fascinating, aren't they?' In her effort to sound at ease she was sounding shrill, and he shrugged.

'You've seen one dark hole, you've seen them all.'

'But the atmosphere——'

'Ah, yes, there's always the atmosphere,' he agreed.

He pushed aside the panel that was the office door, went in and closed it behind him, and Clarry shrugged too, lifting her shoulders high and wriggling away the tension. An awkward situation had been defused because it was nothing anyway. It would send her friends into gales of laughter, but she didn't think she would tell anyone. What she would do was forget it.

Her first chore was brushing down the chimneypiece, in clean white gloves with a white hogshair brush, collecting the dust in a vacuum dustette. She pulled on the cotton gloves and began painstakingly, but within minutes Nicolas Dargan was back.

Seeing how she was treating his chimneypiece was bound to interest him. Perhaps not for long, because it was slow work, but he was watching her every move, standing close behind her, and she thought, If I had a chisel in my hands I could slip with it and do some real damage.

Not much could go wrong with a brush, but she was sure her fingertips were stiffening, and the back of her neck was knotting up, and when she turned and met his heavy-lidded scrutiny she snapped, 'I don't like working with somebody looking over my shoulder. Do you?'

'Makes no difference to me,' he shrugged.

She laughed harshly. 'Come off it! I don't believe you. King of the dodgy deals!'

'Who told you that?' He sounded amused.

'Gets around,' although Nicolas Dargan was generally described as audacious and far-sighted, not dodgy, and he tutted at her as though she was a cheeky child.

'Spreading rumours can be very expensive.'

Clarry knew it would be wiser to shut up, but she couldn't help muttering, 'A really good one might be worth it,' and he said,

'It seems I've got myself a sparring partner after all.' After all the attention he'd paid her yesterday he must be wondering where the rapport had gone. 'Well,' he said with a grim weariness, 'never say I didn't warn you.'

CHAPTER FOUR

WHEN Nicolas Dargan went into the office this time he left the door open. Clarry heard the phone ring and she heard him answer it, and listening to him was almost as bad as having him breathing down the back of her neck.

His voice was deep and carrying. He wouldn't need to raise it to sway a crowd or to be in charge of a board meeting, and she thought sourly, If he should ever start bellowing he'd have them running for cover!

There was no trouble on the phone; things seemed to be going well with whoever it was who had rung this number. Nicolas sounded amiable, but Clarry made a move to shut the door panel. Then she stopped herself. The office was small, it could be oppressive for such a big man, and she could hardly explain that something about his voice was really getting to her.

Everything would be easier when she was through in here. She finished the initial dusting of the chimneypiece and began to check for tiny cracks and roughness of salt formation under the undercut sections; and all the while she was conscious of his nearness. He was dictating now, and although his voice was hardly more than a murmur he made her so tense that the muscles across her shoulderblades were literally aching.

It was a gloomy day. She hadn't noticed that particularly until he came out again, and again stood watching her. Then she said, 'You're in my light.'

'Switch the lights on,' he said, reasonably enough.

There were wall brackets, most of the ceilings were too low for anything else, and she complained, 'Now I'm in your shadow.'

'That,' he said, 'is your problem,' and as soon as he walked out of the room Clarry came out of the spell.

It *was* like a spell, as if his voice stirred dark memories, and his shadow lay heavy on her. She could only work comfortably when he was nowhere near, and she wasted no time for the rest of the morning. For lunch she got sandwiches from the kitchen and worked while she ate. By mid-afternoon she was testing the stone for porousness and applying one of Danny's pastes to tar stains.

Paul Burnley found her doing that when he came looking for her with the photographs. He had taken the film for developing at breakfast time, and when the door of the King's Room opened she thought at first that Nicolas Dargan was back. She would rather see anyone else, and she gave the agent a welcoming smile and put down her tools.

The photographs had come out clearly, showing what they were supposed to show. They discussed them for a few minutes, then she asked him, 'Where's the priest's hole? It wouldn't be in the room I have?'

She would have liked that, but he told her, 'It's in a store-room—would you like to see it?'

'Yes, please.' She could do with a break, and she was fascinated by the hiding place that had saved a king.

The store-room in the attics was almost filled with packing cases. Paul hauled one out of a corner, and the floorboards beneath were old and gnarled. It was hard even now to make out a trapdoor. When it was first constructed it would have been completely concealed. He raised the flap on the blade of a Swiss pocket knife, high enough for a fingertip hold, then lifted it up for Clarry to peer in.

It wasn't a bad size. Charles had been six feet tall, head and shoulders above the average for those days.

The wooden seat left room to stretch your legs and he could have stood almost upright, but everyone must have held their breath while the King hid here and the soldiers tramped through the house.

As Clarry stared down entranced Paul Burnley suggested, 'Try it,' and she swung herself down on to the seat. As she sat he explained, 'It bolts on the inside, otherwise the weight kept it shut.'

He was holding the lid, and she put up her hands and he let her take the weight. It was heavier than she expected, pushing her down and slamming, plunging her into blackness with no glimmer of light.

Ever since the time of her coma darkness had terrified her, and now she was gasping for breath as if she was strangling, sagging against the wall with no more strength in her limbs than she had had when she opened her eyes in her sickbed.

Then blessed light flooded in, and Paul Burnley's pleasant blunt-featured face swam above her.

'Not bad, is it?' he said cheerily. 'No light, but air gets in. It might get claustrophic after a while, but it was a good hiding place.' Clarry still couldn't move, and his cheerfulness went. 'Are you all right?' he asked anxiously.

'Help me out,' she gasped.

He had to jump down and lift her, and when she managed to lurch to her feet her teeth were chattering. 'Sorry—I'm claustrophobic. The door slipped.'

Now he was all concern and apology. 'I thought you'd shut it to get the feel,' he explained. It could only have been closed for seconds, but that was long enough to take her back to some deep dark haunted place, and leave her nauseous even while she was gasping, 'I'm all right now.'

'Sure?'

'I could do with some air,' she admitted.

There was dust up here and her stomach was heaving. Paul put an arm round her and she stumbled down the staircase, coming face to face with Nicolas Dargan on the first floor. 'Clare's feeling faint,' Paul declared.

Nicolas said nothing. Neither did his expression, except that he was waiting for further explanation.

'It was the priest hole,' said Paul, and Nicolas said smoothly,

'She seems to have trouble with priests' holes. She should stick to chimneypieces.'

Get on with her work, he meant, and stop fooling about, and Clarry wondered what would happen if she told Paul Burnley, 'I was looking for one in the King's Room this morning and I came on this character stark naked. A sight to give anybody claustrophobia!' Not on, but tempting.

She had stopped shaking. A flare of temper had done her a power of good. She had worked through her lunch hour; why shouldn't she take ten minutes off? She smiled at the estate manager and said, 'Thank you so much. Sorry about this, and I really am fine now.'

Nicolas held the door of the King's Room open for her. She said sweetly, 'See you later,' to Paul Burnley and went in. Nicolas followed her and closed the door behind him. She didn't look at him. She went to the photographs she had left on an oak chest and began sorting out the shots of this fireplace, and he said:

'Burnley's a good lad, but in some aspects he's inexperienced. Don't take advantage of him.'

That made her look up and yelp, 'That's rich, coming from you! You take advantage, don't you?'

'I'm employing him.'

'Of course you are.' Her voice rose. '*And* you're employing me.' She glared. 'As Rickard Restoration, and damn all else!'

She felt like an angry cat, spitting and showing its claws, and he got a half smile, that was only a quirk of an eyebrow and a hint of laughter in the voice. 'What else did you think I had in mind for you?' he drawled. 'Apart from a sparring partner?'

Too uneven a contest, he had said, and in a fight she would be no match. They stood apart now, as though they measured each other, and Clarry wondered, Where the hell are your weak points?

He confused her and he angered her, but she would never underestimate his power. He must be so used to exerting it, charming and using, and if that failed dealing as he did with Nigel... 'Do as I say or else...'

'By the way, what happened with the priest's hole just now to have you tottering downstairs in Burnley's arms?' he asked.

'I was shut in,' she explained.

'How long for?'

'No time really,' she admitted. 'A few seconds.'

'But long enough for the atmosphere to get you?' His amusement was sardonic now. 'You are a sensitive plant!' and she said:

'I used to be, but I got tougher when I got this.'

She touched the white streak in her hair, and he drawled, 'My advice to you is to dye that, before you develop a fixation on it.'

'When I want your advice——'

'You'll ask for it,' he finished.

'Don't hold your breath!' she snapped.

'Don't be childish.'

She thought, You've changed your tune from when I was 'all woman', but she was sounding brash, and she turned back to the photographs and was very relieved when Nicolas walked out.

There was plenty still to be done on this fireplace, but tomorrow she would start on something else so that when he was in here she could keep out. Being near him was causing her stress she did not need.

While she was alone she worked fast and efficiently, and a couple of hours passed before she had another interruption.

Fiona Stretton could have stepped out of a fashion magazine, and Clarry could understand why she kept her distance. Pale blue trousers and pale blue cashmere sweater, perfectly matching pale blue eyes, might have been contaminated by dusty dungarees, although she was making quite a show of keeping clear of the fireplace and Clarry, edging round the room.

'Hi,' said Clarry. 'He isn't in.'

She presumed Fiona was heading for the office, but she stopped now and brushed an invisible fleck from her sleeve, then demanded, 'How well do you know Nicolas?'

The question was curt, and Clarry muttered, 'Better than most.' She had had experience of Nicolas Dargan at his roughest and toughest, and it would surprise her if Fiona Stretton had.

'And that's why you got this job?' Fiona was looking at Clarry with a disdain bordering on contempt, and that was downright stupid.

If she had been different Clarry could have told her, 'Somebody recommended me to the estate manager. Nicolas knew nothing about it.' As it was, Clarry was in no mood to reassure Fiona Stretton about anything.

'Could be,' she said, and left it at that, and Fiona began to view the chimneypiece, her expression rapidly becoming super-critical.

In its unfinished state it was patchy. 'I only hope you know what you're doing,' she said, as if she doubted that, and Clarry acted puzzled.

'Are you talking about chimneypieces or Cole Dargan?'

'It's Cole, is it?' Fiona's lips had thinned. 'I'm talking about the fireplace, of course. How's it going to look when you've finished. Like new?'

'No,' said Clarry. If it did it would stick out like a sore thumb. The stone had mellowed and aged with the rest of the house. Did the girl think she was going to scour it down?

Fiona gave a little sigh and said coldly, 'You may be here because you and Nicolas are old friends——' Clarry opened her mouth and closed it '—but our standards are very high.'

'*Our* standards?' Clarry acted dumb again. 'Do you mean yours? And I thought we were being employed by Dargan Enterprises.'

Fiona brushed that aside. 'Of course you are, but if your work is second-rate Nicolas won't let sentiment sway him.'

She was so obnoxious, she was ridiculous, and Clarry drawled, 'But everybody knows that sentiment never enters into a Dargan deal. I quite understand that—I always have.'

Nigel could have been different, but Nigel was never the boss nor likely to be, and Clarry had had enough of Miss Fiona rabbiting on. 'And I tell you what I think you should do now,' she said as if a bright idea had just struck. 'You'll find Danny Hill in the drawing-room or somewhere around. He's my right-hand man, and he'll be doing a great deal of work here. Why don't you run along and tell *him* that you and Cole Dargan expect us to keep up the standards you're both accustomed to?'

If Fiona was stupid enough to do that Danny might not say much, but his response would be blistering. His reputation must have reached Fiona somehow, because she said quickly, 'I think you should speak to him,' and Clarry grinned.

'I bet you do,' she said.

She watched Fiona flounce out of the room and did a little deep breathing before she returned to her assault on the tar stains. Paul Burnley was right—Miss Fiona was a spoiled bitch. She deserved to get Nicolas Dargan, but on the whole Clarry did not think she would, because the last thing he was was a fool.

* * *

Night was falling when she finished for the day and the house was filling with shadows. Danny was in the parlour with a newspaper, and she gave him the photographs, then rang her work number from a phone on the ground floor and listened to several messages that had come on to her answerphone that day. There was nothing too urgent, and after today a friend who ran a mobile catering business from the next unit would be checking her morning mail for her.

Then she showered in the little bathroom, washing her hair to get rid of the dust, and came downstairs freshened up to join Danny in their evening meal.

The food was good, well cooked and well served, and tonight they ate alone. Paul Burnley didn't join them and Clarry didn't miss him. Danny was comfortable as an old pair of slippers, and it had been a tiring day.

She did all the talking, she always did with Danny. She told him how she was getting on with the chimneypiece. She described the priest's hole in the attic, not getting shut in and panicking but where it was and how it worked. They looked at all the photographs, and she said that Fiona had asked her if the chimneypiece was going to be good as new when it was finished.

Danny looked horrified, and she teased, 'I told her to find you and tell you how she wants the carving done,' and he grinned like a mischievous monkey.

Never once did Clarry mention Nicolas Dargan, so that, listening to her, Danny must have believed she had never set eyes on him today. In fact, from the moment she had opened his bathroom door this morning he was either around, or he might as well have been, because everything that had happened to her since had been dominated by him. If she had told Danny the half of it he would have been worried to death.

As it was, Danny was relaxed enough to eat a good meal and then doze off in an armchair by the fire. At the table Clarry made notes dealing with the answerphone messages, read the newspaper and started the crossword.

When she was home she had a busy social life, but she and Danny often spent evenings alone like this. She was always content to be with the old man who had done more for her than she could ever repay.

This room was about the same size as the living-room in the bungalow. The Lodge was a much grander house, the furniture in here was worth a whole lot more than theirs, but there was a familiar feel about the situation. Clarry often occupied herself while Danny snoozed, and now she solved a crossword clue with a self-satisfied smirk and decided that tomorrow she would see about getting a radio.

It was warm and cosy, with even the right background sounds: a ticking clock and Danny softly snoring. Then the door swung silently open and Nicolas Dargan was framed in the doorway.

He seemed to fill it. Behind him the corridor was darker than the room. The temperature dropped and Clarry imagined that the wind was rising. Enter the demon king, she thought crazily, and snapped, 'Don't you knock on doors?'

This was a sitting-room; why shouldn't anyone walk in? But she had felt a chill when he materialised because she had felt so safe and secure before.

'You're a fine one to talk about knocking first after this morning,' he said, and she hoped she would not have to explain that to Danny. 'We're expecting company—will you both be joining us?'

'Who's coming?' Again she was speaking without stopping to think, because she would hardly be likely to know them, whoever they were.

'Folk from around here, mostly,' he told her.

'Miss Stretton's friends?'

'Most of them.'

Fiona had had no part in this invitation. She wouldn't want Clarry and Danny meeting her friends. Were these the crowd she hoped Nicolas Dargan would meet in the clubhouse yesterday, so that she could show them what a twosome she and he were? Only they were not, because no one was getting that kind of commitment from him.

'Not much for company,' said Danny, as brusquely as if he was being invited to join in an orgy, and Clarry knew why Nicolas wanted his 'old friend Clare' along. She was almost tempted to go, because Fiona Stretton needed taking down a peg, she had been insufferable this afternoon.

Nicolas said nothing. He looked at Clarry as he had that first morning, when she had walked into the King's Room expecting to be sacked before she started, and again it was tunnel vision, so that he was all she could see, and she thought wildly, If he touches me it will be the way it was with the handshake, and heaven help me, I'll go with him.

Somehow she looked away, but it was like tearing herself free. She was surprised when her voice came out so bright and brittle. 'How kind of you to think of us, but I don't think so, thank you—we know our place.'

Nicolas burst out laughing. 'I can't believe I heard that!' He grinned at Danny, who was trying not to grin back. 'If you change your mind——' he said.

'We shan't,' said Clarry. 'Besides, Paul might look in.'

'He won't,' said Nicolas, which could mean the estate manager was joining the guests or working late, but she felt she was being parted from an ally and bit her lip to stop herself asking, How do you know? Have you warned him off me?

As Nicolas closed the door behind him Danny said, 'Keep it to business. Keep out of his way.'

'Don't you worry about that,' Clarry said grimly. 'I'm not likely to forget what I owe to Cole Dargan,' and she thought Danny suddenly looked very old indeed.

She jumped up and went across to him. 'Hey,' she said, 'shall we try to pair him off with Fiona Stretton—don't you think it would serve him right?'

That made Danny smile. 'Pigs might fly,' he said.

But the peace of the evening was shattered for Clarry. Not that there was that much noise. She did hear cars arriving and when she listened carefully she could catch the sound of voices and laughter, but it was in no way a boisterous party.

The main room was beneath this little parlour. Clarry had been in there, and while she sat with the newspaper on the table in front of her she was imagining it now. Panelled walls and oil paintings, red Persian rugs on the dark polished floor, and genuine Jacobean furniture. How much of that

Nicolas Dargan had brought with him and how much the Strettons had sold with the house Clarry didn't know, but Fiona would be at home, and most of the guests would be used to seeing her in this setting.

This was her scene, and there would be no sign tonight of the supercilious young woman who had looked down her neat little nose at Clarry this afternoon. She would be smiling at everyone, showing her neat little teeth and sticking close as a shadow to Nicolas Dargan.

For some reason Clarry was finding the idea of that very irritating. Danny had found himself a book and she pretended to carry on with the crossword, getting tetchier by the minute as time dragged by.

Surely Nicolas's voice would carry from the murmur below? She was almost sure she caught it once or twice, but it was impossible to distinguish words, and of course she was not really listening, much less straining to hear.

But she couldn't get the picture of Fiona out of her mind, and if Danny had not been here, and bound to ask where she was going, she might have strolled into the party and fluttered her eyelashes at Nicolas just to take the smirk off Fiona's face.

But that would be playing his game, and that was the last thing she intended to do. So Fiona could go on impressing her friends and showing him what a perfect partner she could be, and blow the pair of them.

Clarry rather wished Paul Burnley *would* turn up. She would cheerfully have gone with him on his late-night amble round the grounds. Keeping out of the maze, though. 'The next time you get lost in the maze after dark you might meet more than you bargained for,' Nicolas had warned her. Like what? Like him and Fiona, sitting on the stone seat?

Clarry had no idea why that should make her want to throw something smashable at the wall, but it did, and she took a paperback thriller off a shelf and read it doggedly, elbows on the table and hands over her ears. Until Danny yawned and said, 'I'm for bed.'

'Me too,' said Clarry. 'I'll take my book up.'

She took her time undressing and washing, getting her make-up off and brushing her hair.

'My advice to you is to dye that white streak before you develop a fixation on it...' Even when she couldn't hear him she kept remembering what he had said. That could be the start of a fixation, an obsession, and tomorrow when she was less tired and cooler-headed she would check that before it became a habit.

In bed she opened her book and realised she would have to start again from the beginning, because while she was downstairs she had hardly taken in a word she was reading.

She couldn't hear the voices up here. The night was peaceful, there was nothing to disturb her, but she was too restless to fall asleep, and she was still trying to read when the guests started to leave.

They hadn't stayed that late, it was only around eleven o'clock when she heard the first car doors slamming and engines revving up. She switched off her light and opened her window just wide enough to see down into the forecourt and the drive, and then she could hear the voices again.

They all seemed to be leaving at the same time, and from the sound of them it had been a good party as they called and laughed, and streamed around in the lights from the house and the open door.

Clarry watched them going, car after car, until at last there were only two figures down there on the forecourt, Nicolas Dargan, dark in a dark suit, and Fiona with her silver-gilt hair and a pale dress that floated when she turned from waving goodbye to a departing Mercedes and looked up at the man beside her.

She was laughing, Clarry thought, smiling anyway as though it had been a lovely evening, but now they had all gone the best was to come. With her hand through Nicolas's arm they strolled towards the house together, and Clarry instinctively shrank down on her bed, although she could hardly be seen up here.

Reflected light went out on the cobblestones as the heavy main door closed. Now they would be in the entrance hall. Where would they go from there? she wondered. What would they say to each other when there was no other company? What would they do?

She felt terrible, hunched in her bed. She was an outsider here, of course she was, and it shouldn't be bothering her, but suddenly she could have wept into her pillow like a lonely child.

She understood that better in the morning. It was because she was crazy about the house that she envied Fiona Stretton, who was managing to hang on to King's Lodge, not because she was hanging on to Nicolas Dargan down there. Clarry could never be jealous of a man she disliked so heartily, and today she was going to start cleaning the big fireplace in the entrance hall, doing as Danny said and keeping out of his way.

This fireplace was massive. In the old days all the cooking had been done here, cauldrons had simmered, great sides of meat had rotated on spits; but long ago a room leading off the hall had been turned into a kitchen, and now the fireplace was a showpiece on which logs burned on occasions. The fire was out now, although ashes were left piled and a charred log was waiting to be topped with kindling.

After breakfast Clarry went down, carrying a piled tray. Staff were about. There was the hum of a vacuum cleaner, a girl was running a polisher over the quarry-tiled floor, and in the kitchen the housekeeper and the cook were bustling around.

'I'll be working down here this morning,' Clarry told them. 'I'm starting on the main fireplace.'

She crept into the King's Room to get her tools, and again the bed was smooth and the room was empty, and she was not waiting to find out if Nicolas was in the bathroom behind the panelling or not. She grabbed and ran, and came down the stairs clutching her bulky canvas bag.

This time the girl with the polisher, hovering near the chimneypiece, called, 'Sounds as if there's a bird up there.'

'Oh, no!' Clarry went to see. That probably happened quite often with these wide chimneys when there was no smoke rising.

'Usually they get out,' said the girl. 'Could be a bat—more likely a bird, though.'

You could see right to the sky, and high up there the bird was fluttering, beating its wings in frantic flight. Clarry willed it out, standing below with upturned face. If it didn't escape it would fall exhausted, probably with a broken wing, and it was so near the top if it would only fly up instead of thrashing around.

She heard the girl squeak, 'Oh, Mr Dargan!'

She didn't look at him. She felt that the bird was going to make it so long as she didn't take her eyes off it, like cheering on a racer, Come on, you can do it, nearly there! Go, man, *go*! 'What are you looking for now?' Nicolas asked her, and she said, 'Why don't you take a wild guess?' and heard the girl giggle nervously.

Now the bird was silhouetted with wide-spread wings in the circle of white that was the sky, and then it was gone and she cried, 'It's out!' but almost before the words were through her lips a fall of soot from the bird's last brush with the chimney walls came down on her. She had no time to duck away before it had covered head and shoulders like a soft sticky veil, filling her mouth and eyes so that she staggered back, gagging and spluttering.

She heard Nicolas Dargan laugh, right by her, and she lurched against him, rubbing her head on his jacket, burrowing her face into his shirt.

She was blinded. Couldn't see a thing. She could hear the women dear-oh-dearing, and she blinked and gasped, 'Oh, how *awful*! I can't tell you how sorry I am.'

She had managed to transfer a liberal amount of soot. He didn't look quite as bad as she did, but bad enough. 'Don't even try,' he said. 'You'd better get cleaned up.'

'And you.' He probably suspected she had done that deliberately, and she was suddenly aware of his hands on her shoulders and jumped back as if he might start shaking her.

'I'll see you down here in fifteen minutes,' he said. 'Bring a jacket.'

'What for?' Clarry queried.

But he had gone, and someone was handing her a towel, which was fine for mopping off the top layer, but the residue would need soap and hot water. By now most of the staff seemed to be here, and those who had seen what had happened were telling those who had not, 'She fell right up against Mr Dargan—got soot all over him, but he was ever so nice about it.'

He could hardly have cursed her, with that audience, over what appeared to be an accident. No one could prove it wasn't, and she was admitting nothing. She might even apologise again, because she had overreacted and could just have ruined a very expensive jacket.

Her dungarees and sweater were used to rough treatment. She stripped them off, and had to scrub her skin before she creamed it, and went through half a bottle of shampoo washing the tackiness out of her hair.

Of course it took longer than fifteen minutes. Twenty-five minutes later she hurried downstairs, with flushed face and wet heavy hair, and with a mustard-coloured duffel coat slung over her shoulders.

Nicolas was in the hall, talking to the housekeeper. When he saw Clarry he said something to Mrs Haines and came to the foot of the stairs, calling, 'Come on, we're wasting time.'

'Come on where?' Clarry asked.

'There's a sale of garden statuary. We might get something for the maze.'

She could enjoy that. As she followed him she enquired, 'Who else is coming?'

'Do you think you might need a chaperon or a bodyguard?'

'What an idea!' she said, and managed a little laugh for Mrs Haines, who was listening as if she didn't intend missing a word.

Outside, a Range Rover was waiting, and as Clarry climbed in she gulped and said with what she hoped was the right tone of regret, 'Sorry about just now.'

'Like hell you are.' Nicolas turned and looked her full in the face so that she squirmed in her seat. It was no use trying to bluff him after that. She had been rumbled, and she fell back on her only excuse.

'Well, you shouldn't have laughed at me.'

'Why not? It was the funniest thing I've seen in days.'

'You've got a strange sense of humour,' she said drily.

'What would you have done? If I'd been looking up the chimney and got a sootfall? Especially if I'd just snapped your head off over a perfectly inoffensive question?'

She didn't need to consider. 'I suppose I might have found that pretty funny, but I tell you something. I wouldn't have been standing so close when I started laughing at you.'

'Good advice,' he said. 'Next time I'll remember that.'

'You're expecting a next time?'

They were leaving King's Lodge behind, driving along the winding lane that led to the main thoroughfare. 'Aren't you?' he said, and his smile made her smile.

He was watching the road, which was a series of blind bends and so narrow that if two vehicles met one had to back to a pull-in space.

But somehow he watched her too. 'You look as if it took some getting off,' he said. 'You're still damp around the edges.'

Clarry had towelled her hair, but it was wet enough for moisture to be trickling down her forehead. She fished in her pocket for a tissue.

'And if I didn't know better I'd say there was soot on your eyelashes,' he added. She had always had sooty eyelashes. She pretended to squint through them now and shook her head.

'No,' she said. 'All clear.' She was not going to fight him today. She was taking a break from aggro and her spirits were buoyant. 'Where *are* we going?' she asked.

'To see an old garden with some statuary that's going on the market. We're getting a preview.'

'Where is it?'

'South Wales.' That meant a long drive, but she didn't think she would mind that either.

'What sort of thing are you looking for?' she asked.

'Let's wait and see what's on offer.'

She was flattered that he considered her opinion worth having, and she asked, 'Didn't Fiona want to come along? It used to be her maze.'

'And now it's mine,' Nicolas said cheerfully, and she thought, It can't have gone too brilliantly for Fiona last night. She can't know anything about this trip or she wouldn't have me sitting up front. In the back maybe if he'd insisted on bringing me along, but she would have been right beside him.

She found herself grinning like a Cheshire Cat, so that she had to come up with a joke. 'Danny works in stone too. You could have brought him. He appreciates a likely bit of statuary when he sees it.'

'And how does Daniel Hill show approval?' asked Nicolas.

Danny would think she was mad, going off with Nicolas Dargan like this. It was a business trip and she had had no choice, but when she got back he would be very disapproving indeed.

'He smiles,' she said, and Nicolas looked dubious. 'He can smile. Haven't you seen him?' Of course he hadn't. 'Well, I warned you he was awkward,' and she admitted the obvious, 'He isn't a fan of yours.'

'Judge of character, is he, as well as statues?' Nicolas drawled, and she laughed at that.

'Very much so, and when he gets it wrong it takes wild horses to make him admit it.'

'We'll look out for one.' He smiled down at her, and she wondered if she could have been saying that Danny might have the wrong idea about Nicolas Dargan.

She had to relax. She was sitting so close now, brushing against him when she shifted in her seat, conscious of his every controlled move driving the car. If she let his nearness get under her skin, as it had earlier, her nerves would be strung to screaming before they were anywhere near their journey's end.

So she had to loosen up and she did, and they took the motorway under a dark grey sky. Traffic was not too heavy, the great lorries thundered past heading for Swansea and the docks, but the season of tourists and caravanners was over. The car radio played. Clarry listened to music and news, a short story and a chat show, and watched the changing landscape when they left the motorway.

In a strange way she was finding that faint smell of aftershave soothing. As an occasional hint of it reached her she wondered why it was so evocative. If she closed her eyes and breathed deeply it made her feel almost cherished.

Which was crazy, because Nicolas Dargan was the last man alive to be cherishing her, but the clean male aroma was like a strong arm around her, familiar and comforting, and it had to mean she had come across it before.

Not on Nigel, she thought, but maybe somebody she had liked had worn it. Or perhaps she had sniffed it on a toiletries counter one day when she was feeling on top of the world and thought, That's nice, I could fancy that. Elusive and faint, it intrigued her, so that she found it hard not to sniff openly and ask, 'What's your aftershave?'

That seemed too personal in this confined space, as if she was suggesting it was overpowering when it was anything but, and she hid a smile, reflecting that it would be even more impossible to say, 'There's a lot about you that gets my hackles up, but when I breathe in the way you smell I feel as if I'm being stroked very gently.'

The roads were rougher now, between old market towns, as the rising hills became a mountainous panorama. She saw the ruins of a castle or an abbey on a rocky crag, and later they passed a gloomy lake with old quarry workings at its head.

As a sightseeing run it was fascinating, but she was glad when the car drew up in a high street, outside an estate agents and auctioneers in a row of Georgian buildings.

'I'll be right back,' said Nicolas, and while he was gone Clarry flexed her stiffening muscles.

He was back, almost at once, followed by a dapper little man who seemed to be doing a skipping step and was smiling and talking at the same time. So that's what's meant by dancing attendance, Clarry thought, because when Nicolas opened the door and got into the car the man was still burbling on about showing them the way and its being a pleasure and no trouble at all.

'Thank you,' said Nicolas, 'we'll find it.'

'Yes, yes, of course. And you'll be in touch?'

'Almost certainly.'

'You managed to park right outside,' the man said. He sounded as if that surprised him, and Clarry thought, It doesn't surprise me. The Nicolas Dargans of this world can always find a parking space.

She grinned at that, and he asked, 'What's amusing you now?'

She was still smiling, looking back at the man on the pavement who was watching them go. 'There,' she said, 'you do have a fan.'

'He's got property he wants to unload.'

She laughed, 'I didn't think it was your bonny blue eyes.'

'*Blue* eyes?' he echoed.

'Aren't they?'

She knew exactly what colour his eyes were. Nigel had grey eyes that could look blue sometimes, but Nicolas Dargan's were dark as pitch, and they would never change colour. She said impulsively, 'You and Nigel don't even look like cousins.'

'Nevertheless we are. Any bastardy in the family missed our generation.'

'I wasn't suggesting——'

'But you're right, we're not alike. And the difference is rather more than skin-deep.' He spoke quietly, but his voice was cold, and that was the difference. Nigel was all too human, but Nicolas could be rock-hard to the bone, and Clarry didn't need reminding of that.

She hadn't wanted to spoil today, she hadn't meant to bring up Nigel's name. She changed the subject abruptly, asking, 'How far is it?'

'Only about another five miles.'

'Good,' she said, 'I could use a break. I'm setting in a hairpin position.'

'We could stop for a meal.' They were nearly out of the small town and by now it was midday. 'But I'd rather get our inspection over first. It's up in the hills and I don't altogether trust the weather.'

Inside the car she couldn't judge, but looking at the sky this could be one of those days when night came early, and anyhow it would be more fun to go statue-hunting in an old garden. Food could wait, and she would enjoy stopping somewhere on the way home and dining out leisurely. Danny was going to do his Victorian grandfather act whatever time they got back, a few hours would make no difference.

'Yes, let's go on,' she said.

They turned off the road, went through another hamlet of a few houses and what looked like a farmhouse, and took what seemed hardly more than a track, meeting nothing from then on but sheep perched on the hillside like mountain goats. 'You are sure about this?' Clarry queried as they bumped along. 'Maybe we should have brought the guide.'

'Trust me,' said Nicolas, and she pulled a face.

He chuckled. 'You have such a suspicious mind! But we are on the right track. When the house was in its heyday this would be wider, the surface would be kept repaired,' and when she looked out at the ground beneath their wheels she could see the remains of old concrete.

'Old houses, old roads,' she sighed. 'Are you thinking of saving this one?'

'This one is long past saving. I'm here for the garden.'

'Where *is* it?'

'Any minute now.'

It had been built into the mountainside. They came over a ridge and just below the next rise was a plateau, and a building standing in overgrown grounds within a grey snaking wall.

The car stopped outside gates that were high and closed. Clarry opened her own door and jumped down while Nicolas was coming round the car, and it was so quiet that she could hear his soft tread on the grass. The silence was heavy as though everything held its breath, and she almost whispered, 'Who lived here?' although she knew they were quite alone.

The gates were ornately iron-scrolled, secured by a heavy lock and chain, and she half expected the key would refuse to turn, but it slid round smoothly, and as Nicolas took off the lock he answered her, 'One of the ironmasters built himself a home well away from the foundries. After the closures it stayed that way for a while, but there've been probate problems for years. Now the house has been stripped and what's left in the garden is going up for auction.'

The gate swung open. She thought the hinges would creak, but perhaps they had been oiled for the auction. The short driveway to the house was clear enough too, cropped grass grew between the paving stones.

She hesitated, and knew it was a stupid remark when she muttered, 'I hope we're not disturbing anything.'

'Come on, Clarry,' he said, and it was as if she was hearing an echo. Then she was going with him through the gates and ahead of them was the house: windows gone, most of the roof gone, a gaping hole that had once been the ironmaster's front door.

She wondered about him and his family. 'What a grim title—ironmaster,' she said, and thought it wouldn't be too far off the mark for the man striding along beside her.

Again she got that speculative look as if he was reading her mind, and again she felt that she could be colouring up. 'This one had his dream,' he said drily. 'He created quite a garden.'

It was all around them, neglected and overgrown out of recognition. Trees and shrubs planted up here must have been set in soil brought up for the purpose. Most of it had been washed away since, but some roots had been tenacious enough to hold, although the bushes were wild and the trees stunted. There would have been flowers too, especially in summer, but it was late autumn now and years since anyone had tended the garden. All the flowers had gone, and Clarry followed Nicolas down a path of tangled briars and ferns, round the side of the house.

'We should come on the star exhibit somewhere here,' he said.

'And what's that?'

'The ironmaster's pride and joy, apparently.' He stopped. 'This has to be it.'

She peered round him and gasped. 'Wow!'

'I can't see this lot doing much for the maze,' he said.

It was a neo-classical group in stone of half a dozen women with flowing hair and skimpy draperies, sitting in a wide circle, all with downcast eyes.

'They're very thoughtful,' she said. 'What are they supposed to be? Witches?'

'Water nymphs.' They were more like nymphs than witches; they all had the same simper. But set here among the bracken and the broom...

'*Water*?' she queried.

'I'm told there was a small lake. They're weatherbeaten now, but when they were new and the sun was shining they might have brightened up the ironmaster's outlook.'

So that was what they were doing, admiring their reflections in the lake. 'I'm glad you told me that,' she said. 'I wondered if they were watching for something to come up out of the ground. Which will you have if you decide on them? There wouldn't be room for more than a couple in the maze, would there?'

'You'd be hard pressed to choose. They're all the same, give or take the odd broken finger, and that poor girl who's lost the tip of her nose.'

She went closer to see and declared, 'You should have a fellow feeling for her, with a broken nose, but I think it's an improvement here. They've all got the old Grecian nose; hers is much nicer.'

'Good for her,' said Nicolas, 'but I don't want any of them.'

'What a rotten thing to say! Never mind, girls,' she told them gaily, 'there are those who will appreciate you.' They were hardly works of art, but they would probably sell at the auction. 'Although you might be split up,' she added.

'That's not going to worry them.' He moved away from the circle across what might have been a tennis court. 'They're a narcissistic bunch. All they'll need is a mirror each.'

'What *are* you looking for?' He probably had something in mind to have dismissed the water nymphs out of hand, and he was striding purposefully now through a rusting iron archway and into a copse.

Over his shoulder he told her, 'There was a set of King's Beasts, from the same quarry as the water babes. Most of them are still around.'

'The lion and the unicorn,' Clarry quoted.

'That's right.'

Either would be splendid, and searching for mythical beasts in a secret garden was magical. This must have been a place of fantasy on the mountainside when the house was a home. She could imagine the lake, fed from mountain streams, the arbours, the flower beds, the rock gardens and dells. There were still paved paths beneath the turf, and she was picking her way carefully down a shallow flight of moss-covered steps when Nicolas said, 'This should be the pillar garden.'

'Pillow?'

'Pillar. Trees were the pillars; it was a terrace.'

Left to their own devices, the trees were no longer in neat straight rows. Some had died off, some had grown gnarled, and what must have been a smooth-lawned walk between them had gone back to scrubland. But it was still the lair of the beasts.

The first beast was by the first tree, sitting up on its hind legs in the pose of a begging dog. But this was no dog, this was a battered bull, lurching slightly where the ground had subsided.

It was nearly as tall as Clarry, and she turned eagerly to Nicolas. 'But he's marvellous! You'll never do better than him. He's the next best thing to a Minotaur——' the half bull, half man that roamed the legendary maze of ancient Crete, and Nicolas laughed.

'You want the Minotaur? When they got to the middle of his maze he ate them.'

'I'd forgotten that, but this one looks friendly enough.'

'All the same, we'll see them all.'

Clarry could see more, and she said happily, 'It's like coming across a lost city—weird and wonderful. I'm so glad you brought me. How many are there?'

'There should be ten. Some have gone.'

'I hope the unicorn's still here.' Nicolas was standing back now, while she was darting backwards and forwards over the rough ground searching for the unicorn.

She found a lion and a dragon, and what looked like a horse but for the broken stub of a single horn, and she called, 'I've found it!' He came then, and she said, 'A unicorn would be stunning.'

'See the rest first.'

The figures were mostly at drunken angles. One had toppled over, dragging the roots of a small tree with it, and she knelt down by it. Then she sat back on her heels and squealed, 'You'll never guess what this one is!'

'What?'

'A *griffin*!' She had told him about the griffin Danny had carved for her, but she didn't expect him to remember. 'They're very rare,' she said, 'but I've got one in olivewood at home that I'm very fond of. Don't you think this one's handsome?'

Nicolas bent over it with her, and it was a nightmarish creature. 'No,' he said, but he was smiling, and she pressed on,

'That's because you're not looking at it the right way. Griffins are a marvellous mixture. The head of an eagle and the body of a lion—how's that for a winning combination? Sounds rather like the kind of man I've been looking for,' she joked, and he chuckled.

'With wings?' A winged monster, was the griffin.

'Optional extra, but wings have got to be wonderful.' Clarry was talking such nonsense.

'Not always,' he said. 'If you fly you can fall.'

There was a great crack through the wing on which the statue was lying, and she touched it gently. 'Looks as if he did.'

'That could be repaired.'

'Of course it could. Can we take the griffin?'

'We can.'

She jumped to her feet, alight with delight, and when he held out a hand to steady her she clung to him, laughing. 'Who'd have thought there'd be a griffin here? Did you know there might be a griffin?'

Danny's gift had been waiting for her on her birthday morning, and none of the other presents had thrilled her like the beautiful little carving. Danny knew it was her favourite of everything he had made for her. He had placed it by her bedside five years later so that it was one of the first things she saw when she came out of her coma.

Now the same youthful elation of her fourteenth birthday had her practically flinging her arms around Nicolas Dargan and exclaiming, 'Thank you!'

This griffin was no gift, but when he said, 'You're welcome,' it seemed as if it was. Then he kissed her forehead lightly, and it meant nothing except that their search had gone well and her exuberance was amusing him. But she wished he would kiss her mouth, because, against all her instincts and her better judgement, she seemed to be losing her inhibitions where Nicolas Dargan was concerned.

CHAPTER FIVE

WATCH it, Clarry warned herself. It was one thing to hug Nicolas Dargan in the excitement of the moment, but very much another to let him guess that if he had kissed her harder or longer her knees would have given way.

When she moved he let her go at once—he had hardly been holding her, she had been doing the clinging—and she turned back to the fallen statue, keeping her voice light. 'That's it, then, I suppose. We go away and leave him here and you tell them you want him.' She tugged at a brittle root around the base as if she was trying to free the griffin, and admitted, 'I'll be sorry to leave him behind.'

'We can always take him with us,' said Nicolas.

'How?' This was several hundredweight of rock up a mountainside they were talking about. 'He's too heavy to move, let alone carry.'

'We'll get help. Trust me.'

He was smiling, and she said gaily, 'Well, it was the right track, so of course I trust you,' and she knew that if Danny could have heard her he would have said, You're out of your mind, girl!

They went back the way they came, past the simpering sisters, through the gates to the car. The air was no longer still, little gusts of wind eddied around them, and Clarry wondered what it would be like up here when night came down.

While Nicolas was talking on the car phone she stood with her hands deep in the pockets of her duffel coat, looking through the open gates at the shell of the house. There would be no moon or stars tonight, the clouds were too heavy, and although it was still early afternoon she had been stupid wanting to wait until the griffin was uprooted and shipped down the mountainside.

That would take time, and the rough ground would be a hazard. When she had said she was sorry to leave the statue behind she hadn't expected Nicolas to say, 'We'll take it with us,' as if it was as easy as loading something you'd bought in the high street into the boot of your car.

She turned from the gate, as he put down the phone and leaned across to open the passenger door for her. 'Do you think this is a good idea?' she asked. 'I mean, there's no urgency, he isn't going anywhere, he could be collected any time. I'm being a nuisance, aren't I?'

She was in the car and as she closed the door he said, 'I'll give you that. You can be a nuisance.'

'So, stop them.'

'But not at the moment.'

He must mean over Nigel, when briefly she had presented him with a problem, and she said tartly, 'I'm thrilled to know I'm not being a nuisance today. That really gives me a boost.'

'Not after the sootfall,' he said drily.

'Are we talking about that? I thought we were talking about Nigel.'

'There too. You have a talent for disruption.'

At least she wasn't boring him, and she asked, 'Are you getting a removal gang?'

'They're on their way,' he told her.

'How are they coming?' She looked up. 'By helicopter out of the clouds? Are they going to pluck him up and carry him off?'

'No. By tractor up the hill. They'll dig him out and cart him down on to level ground and into our car.'

Put like that it seemed simple enough, but it needed someone with Nicolas Dargan's reputation to get this speed of action. He had probably rung the man with the statues and property to sell, who was anxious to oblige in any way. 'There's Dargan clout for you,' said Clarry.

'Don't knock it,' he said. 'It has its uses.'

'I know, I know. You not only have a talent for stirring things, you've got the big guns to back you up.'

'Something else we have in common: we're both stirrers.' And somehow she was leaning against him, in the crook of his arm again with her head on his shoulder, as she had in the little green room at the heart of the maze. But this seat was softer and it was warmer, and it was a pleasant place and a pleasant way to wait.

Nicolas's jacket was dark grey, smooth against her cheek with the hardness of his broad shoulder beneath it. She remembered the coat she had buried her sooty face in had been a lighter colour, and she wondered if she should offer to get the soot marks off. She was good with stains, but she was sure his jacket would be professionally cleaned without her assistance.

Her eyelids were getting heavier and she stifled a yawn. 'Lack of food?' he asked.

She was not all that hungry. 'Not really,' she said. 'Just comfortable.'

'Go to sleep, I'll wake you when the back-up team arrives.'

He turned on the radio and there was atmospheric crackle, and she thought he turned if off again, because she did doze, curled up like a kitten against him.

When he touched her cheek and said, 'They're here,' she looked up into his face and was glad to see him.

'Hello,' she said. 'How long have I been asleep?'

'Hardly any time. We've got an express service.'

Clarry sat upright. A farm tractor and a trailer were drawing up behind the car and three small wiry men jumped down as Nicolas got out and went to meet them. Clarry followed. Unlike the Dargans, there was a strong family likeness here; they had to be father and sons, and they had been briefed on what was wanted.

'One of the beasts, is it?' said Father. 'Let's be seeing it, then,' and he walked ahead with Nicolas while his sons unhitched the trailer and dragged it along between them.

Father did the talking. He remembered the garden when it was a pretty place, but a man who expected to keep it blooming up here must have taken his brains off with his bowler. It was always a daft notion, and now the house was as good as gone and another few years all that would be left would be a few old bricks and stones.

He sounded as if that had been bound to happen from the start, and Clarry could imagine the locals shaking their heads when the ironmaster first arrived here with his crazy dreams.

Reaching the pillar garden, the trailer was carried and hauled over the scrub until it was set down beside the griffin. Father and sons looked at each other. They knew all that was left in the garden, and the griffin seemed to be nobody's favourite. 'He's a chiller,' said Father. 'And this is the one the lady wants?'

Clarry had hurried ahead so that she was standing by the griffin before they were. Now she said, 'Yes, please.'

'And she wants to take it home with her?' The older son spoke for the first time.

'That's what she wants,' said Nicolas, and the men looked at him with fellow feeling. They might not know who Nicolas Dargan was, except that it would be worth their while to get that monster out of the old garden for him, but Clarry guessed they had women in their lives who could surprise them. No accounting for women's tastes, their expressions said, and a man like the big man here could probably afford to humour a whim.

They thought she had done the choosing—in a way she had—and that this was being delivered to her home that was probably his home. Which it was for the next few weeks, but it was hysterical that they were seeing her as a woman whose wish was Nicolas Dargan's command.

She couldn't resist giving him a swift teasing glance as they began unloading the trailer. 'I don't know what they imagine my role is here,' she whispered.

'Oh yes, you do,' he said. 'And they don't think much of your choice of statues either.'

'Can I help it if I fancy beasts?'

'That's a loaded question, I'll need notice of that.' They smiled at each other, and Clarry tossed her hair back and felt the wind lifting it like a caress as she looked up at him. This had been a day to remember. With anyone else the old garden would have been interesting, but Nicolas put an edge on everything as though she was waltzing through a wonderland. 'Make yourself useful,' he said. 'Hold my coat.' He took it off and handed it to her. 'No sense ruining two jackets on the same day.'

'Are you digging?' she asked. They had picks and spades, something that looked like a cutter, ropes and sacking.

'Of course I'm digging, they're not needing a foreman.'

Father measured him up, a giant of a man who looked as if he could handle himself or anything else, and enquired, 'Don't mind getting your hands dirty, sir?'

'It won't be the first time,' said Nicolas, 'or the last.'

'Right then,' said Father. 'You can get on to the roots and we'll start clearing the ground.'

The uprooted tree was dead, but the tangle was dense around the base. Some roots Nicolas cut with the cutter, others he tore away, while the men worked on the undergrowth. It must have been quite a while since the griffin had tumbled, it was firmly embedded, and Clarry itched to get in there herself and move something, but they were doing too well as a team to make room for her.

They dug and dragged and grunted and heaved, and under the scrub great clumps of earth cracked and resisted like rock. But at last they had ropes underneath, hauling and shoving until they rolled it aside towards the sacking that was spread out.

Insects scuttled and swarmed, and Clarry kept well back until the displaced homesteaders had been brushed off, most of them with a large white handkerchief by Nicolas.

The broken wing was left behind. While the men, lifting together, were getting the main figure into the trailer and roping it securely, she grubbed away beside the wing, down on her knees, until Nicolas picked her up bodily. 'Out of the way, girl!'

A temper spark glinted in her eyes. She resented being set unceremoniously aside, no matter how goodhumouredly it was done, and she snapped, 'Who do you think you are—Danny?'

'Danny wouldn't care for that comparison. If you don't want a one-winged griffin, let's get the rest of him aboard,' said Nicolas calmly.

She noticed again how grimy and sweat-stained they all were. They wanted the job finished and she was getting in their way, but she said, 'If there'd been another shovel I could have done more than just stand around holding your coat.'

She wasn't doing even that now. She had dropped it, but she picked it up again and shook off the twigs and loose grasses, and Father said encouragingly, 'Of course you could,' and to Nicolas, 'You've got a very willing young lady here.'

'I appreciate that,' said Nicolas, and Clarry managed to say,

'Only with shovels,' before she burst out laughing.

Getting the trailer, with the griffin aboard, back to the tractor, was sweatingly hard work. The sheep farmers—by now names had been swapped, and that was their farm at the bottom of the track—were tough. They could have managed on their own, but the muscle power of the fourth man was a mighty help, and Nicolas Dargan hauled with the best of them.

Paul Burnley, who had told Clarry, 'There's a reserve about him...nobody gets familiar with him,' would hardly have recognised his boss; but the estate manager only knew the tycoon, the ice-cool manipulator with nerves of steel, and Nicolas was all of that.

But there was no restraint about him now. He was mucking in, pulling his considerable weight, talking with the men in Welsh, to Clarry's astonishment. She did a double-take and listened carefully before she was sure.

Back at King's Lodge they only saw him immaculate and expensively dressed, the way most folk must see him. Now he could have been all-in wrestling on a dirt track, she was glad he was helping to bring the griffin down, and she thought he looked incredibly sexy, sleeves rolled up, tie and collar pulled loose.

When the trailer was hitched to the tractor she had a mad urge to run her fingers through his hair and pretend to straighten his tie. But she didn't think he would care for that, so she restrained herself to handing over the jacket and saying, 'You could use a wash and brush-up.'

They were all filthy. Clarry had black earth grimed under her own fingernails from her brief scrabbling around the wing, and Nicolas said, 'We're cleaning up at the farm.'

She opened the car door for herself and got in as he said, 'We'll follow you,' and Bryn Thomas, with sons Ralph and Mansell, climbed aboard the tractor, taking a wide turn to get it and the trailer ahead for the ride down the mountainside.

Clarry inspected her nails and asked, 'Who gets the bathroom first?' Going by need, she was low on the list. The men all needed showers or baths, but she could make do with a kitchen sink. 'Do they all live at the farm?'

'Ralph does. Mansell's married, he has one of the houses nearby.' Nicolas had been getting his information while they had been talking in what to her was a foreign tongue. 'But Bryn's wife does bed and breakfasts, so there should be washing arrangements.'

'*Bed* and breakfast?' Clarry gasped before she could stop herself.

'In our case a wash and a meal and on our way.'

He was laughing at her, and she said, 'Of course,' and looked away from him, out of the window where the heavy clouds were breaking up, scudding in the wind. 'I'll clean up easily enough,' she said, 'but you're going to need a lot of hot water.'

'Come here.' He turned her towards him, cupping her chin in one hand, rubbing a grimy fingertip over her cheeks and dabbing her nose. 'That's better.'

'Is that for the soot?' she managed to joke.

'No, that's for me. A little mud suits you.' He reached to get a tissue and remove some of the grime from his hands before starting up the engine and following the tractor.

She could still feel his touch. When he had held her and raised her face to his her bones had liquefied. Odd things were happening to her today, and she wondered, 'What would they say back at King's Lodge if they could see us now?'

She looked all right, her turbulence was under the skin, but on the surface Nicolas Dargan looked rough. 'Paul Burnley wouldn't believe it,' she said.

He shrugged as if what the estate manager believed hardly mattered, and she added mischievously, 'And I don't think Miss Stretton would approve.'

'Don't you?' Of course she wouldn't, although she would be sugar-sweet to his face, looking daggers at Clarry when he was not watching her. Right now Fiona Stretton seemed as unreal as Paul Burnley, faint and faraway like characters in an old black and white film.

Then Nicolas said, 'That leaves Danny Hill.' Danny was real and he would be waiting. 'And I'll deliver you back to him in pristine condition.'

Clarry pulled a face. 'Sounds like a detergent ad! Whiter than white.'

'Pure and uncorrupted.'

'Oh, that's me all right.' It was all a joke, but there had been no serious lovemaking since Nigel had edged himself out of her life. She was working hard these days, but she still had time for friends and fun, and she was never short of admirers. But no physical affairs. That white streak might be a warning against taking another chance on love, but quite simply she had never met a man who could put her beyond the reach of reason, where she stopped thinking and gave herself up to sensation.

Not until now. But bumping along the rock road beside Nicolas Dargan, every time she lurched against him a pulse of pleasure throbbed in her throat and her wrists and deep down inside her. She would have liked to slip her hand through his arm and press close to him.

That was what Fiona was doing last night, in the courtyard after the guests had gone. And into the house probably and heaven knew how long after, while Clarry, in her attic room and her lonely bed, experienced the cold sickness of jealousy for first time in her life.

She had envied Fiona because Nicolas was with her, but he was with Clarry now, and she was learning a lot about him today. She said, 'I didn't know you spoke Welsh.'

'Why should you?' And there was no answer to that.

'How many languages do you know?' she asked.

'Enough to usually follow what's going on.'

'I believe that,' she said, and she thought, I don't want you knowing what's going on with me, that I'm fancying you rotten.

Nicolas liked her, he might fancy her, but if he did it would be temporary, and she would be wiser and safer to put a damper on sexual stirrings that could burn her up if she let them get out of control.

Just ahead of them the trailer's load rolled in its sacking under the binding ropes, and she said, 'I feel as if we're coming back from an expedition bringing treasure.'

'So we are. He'll look magnificent.'

'He'll enjoy living in the maze after all those years with his face in the mud.'

'You've made an old griffin very happy,' he told her.

She said impulsively, 'It made me happy, finding him and you saying you'd have him.'

'You're welcome,' he said again.

Only last night she had said to Danny, 'I'm not likely to forget what I owe to Nicolas Dargan,' for taking Nigel away. But today he couldn't have been kinder. The Thomases, father and sons, thought she was the girl in his life, and it was fun to pretend to herself that she was, for a little while.

They drove into the hamlet to the five-barred farm gate. Beside the gate was a white post that would carry a 'Bed and Breakfast' sign during the holiday months. Now the chains swung empty in the wind and the whole effect was rather gibbet-like, but the gate was opened by a smiling woman who looked pleased they were here.

Bryn Thomas introduced her, 'This is Megan. Meg, Miss Rickard and Mr Dargan. They'll be wanting a bath and a meal—we can go to that, can't we?'

'Oh yes,' said Megan. She had a pretty lilting voice and she was still a pretty woman, plump and dimpled, and her eyes lit appreciatively at the sight of Nicolas. 'No trouble at all,' she said. 'What you got, then?' she asked her husband. Mr Mansell and Ralph were undoing the rope to transfer the griffin, and Bryn unwrapped it so that she could see.

She looked disappointed. 'Oh, yes—well, very nice.'

'Miss Rickard chose it,' said Ralph, the younger son, who had his mother's twinkling eyes.

'Very nice,' Megan repeated. The wind was rising now so that even down here it nearly had Clarry off her feet. Nicolas caught her and got her back on balance.

'Get inside,' he said.

Megan's skirts were flapping round her legs and she put her hands on her dark curly hair as if it was a hat that might blow away. 'Come in, my dear,' she said to Clarry, and drew her through a door that opened into a kitchen.

Clarry was almost breathless, even from that brief buffeting, and she gasped what any fool could see, 'There's quite a gale blowing up!'

'There is that,' Megan agreed. 'I was glad to see the lads coming. It's no place to be up there when it's gale force.' She gave Clarry a knowing grin. 'Although that man of yours looks as if he could stand up to a fair old battering!'

Clarry smiled, 'He could take some shifting.' That little protective move just now had given Megan Thomas the wrong idea too, and it was easy to enter into the spirit of the thing, pretending that Nicolas was her man, although he would have done the same for anyone who had gone spinning in front of him.

Megan switched on lights as they went, leading the way upstairs and past a number of closed doors. This was a good-sized house. If there were only three of them living here there would be room for tourists, and in the summer it would be brighter and warmer. There was a chill in the air now, and when Megan opened the door of a bathroom it looked clean and cold and unused.

She got a towel out of a cupboard. 'I'll get you some soap,' she said, 'and I'll put a match to the fire in the dining-room.' She was back with the soap almost before Clarry was out of her coat. 'I pretty it up,' she said. 'Pink curtains and mats and that. I wasn't expecting anyone, you see.'

'It's lovely,' said Clarry. 'Thank you.'

Everything was lovely today. Finding the griffin was like being granted a wish. It meant there would always be something to remind Nicolas Dargan of her, after the work was done and she and Danny had driven away in their blue and gold van.

It even meant that she could come back to King's Lodge. It shouldn't be too hard to find out when Nicolas was at home, and she could say, 'I was passing by and I dropped in to say hello to the griffin.'

The water was warm, not hot but warm enough to get the grime out of her fingernails. She didn't let it run, it was going to be in demand from other taps, but she washed her hands and her face and then went slowly about getting the tangles out of her hair with a wide-toothed comb and using the limited make-up she carried in her purse—a lipstick and a mascara wand.

She had brushed the mud marks off the knees of her jeans, and this was the best she could do. When she looked at her reflection she thought she had often looked worse, and she knew why her eyes were brilliant and her lips curved in a pussycat smile.

I look like the cat with the cream, she thought; or in this case the girl with the griffin. But it isn't the griffin. It's being here with Nicolas that's lighting me up like a Christmas tree. I can't wait to go downstairs and join him, talk to him, laugh with him, touch him. It was crazy but it was exciting, and she walked along the corridor and down the stairs feeling absurdly happy.

Megan came out of the kitchen, wearing an overall now, and said apologetically, 'I've lit the fire for you, but it'll take a while to warm up.'

The dining-room also had an air of being out of business for the winter. It was a big room and would have looked out up to the rising hills if it had not been getting dark out there. A central light burned and in the tiled fireplace a fire was still smoking and sullen.

A sideboard, a standard lamp, two armchairs near the window and half a dozen tables with chairs furnished it. On summer mornings, with holidaymakers tucking into their breakfasts, it would be a cheerful place, but now it was uninviting and cheerless. Clarry dropped her duffel coat on to one of the armchairs, although if the room didn't warm up she would be wearing it again. Her teeth were starting to chatter and she thought, I hope we're getting hot soup or something.

A phone rang and stopped ringing and she wondered if she should phone the Lodge and ask to speak to Danny. The housekeeper had heard Nicolas telling Clarry they were going to a sale of garden statuary, but not where it was. Danny might be worrying about her not getting back before now. But somebody must know about the Welsh ironmaster's garden, Paul Burnley probably, and Nicolas would think she was fussing, and there was always the car phone. She could get through on that on the way home.

She heard Nicolas's voice and another man's, then Bryn opened the door and both men stood in the doorway surveying the bleakness of the room. 'We eat in the kitchen,' said Bryn. 'You're very welcome to join us.'

'Thank you, we will,' said Nicolas, and Clarry remembered that it had been warm walking into the kitchen, and she had had an impression of shining copper pans and chairs around a big table as Megan guided her through.

Megan was in there now, stirring a saucepan on an old Aga stove. The smell was appetising and two more chairs were pulled up, and Clarry and Nicolas sat down with what was left these days of the Thomas family in the family home.

'Just the two, we've got,' Megan told Clarry. 'Mansell and Ralph, and Mansell's got his own home now. Bryn was one of ten, so they needed all the bedrooms then, I can tell you! Would you have——?' She looked at Clarry's ringless hand. 'No, I suppose not. No?'

'No,' said Clarry.

'Ah, well, plenty of time for that,' said Megan, and Clarry concentrated on a spicy potato soup, anxious not to catch Nicolas's eye.

He looked almost immaculate again, although the shirt under the jacket had to be dingy. The old Windsor armchair was big enough to seat him comfortably. The fare of soup and a Welsh hotpot followed by blackberry and apple pie was excellent, and Megan blushed prettily when he told her so.

He ate heartily and he seemed at home, almost like one of the family. I suppose when you've manhandled a monster down a mountainside together it's bound to give you a fellow feeling, Clarry thought; because Nicolas Dargan and the Thomas men were getting along famously.

Ralph was talking now almost as much as his father, ranging from Welsh international rugby football to what was going on locally. All the Thomases seemed to have the gift of the gab, Nicolas Dargan could be good company in any gathering, and it was all relaxed and convivial.

When the talk came round to the sale of the statues they felt they knew Clarry well enough to tell her what they thought of her choice. 'What are you going to do with a thing like that?' Megan asked, and she said,

'Put him in a garden.'

'Not my garden!' Megan gave a little shudder. 'Give me the creeps, he would! Tell you what I do fancy, though. One of the girls. Look very nice on the patio, one of the girls would.'

Bryn shook his head. 'I don't know about that. Depends what they're asking for them.' Clarry could see him wondering if he should ask Nicolas what he was paying for the griffin, and thought it unlikely that a price had been fixed. Nicolas Dargan of Dargan Enterprises took what he wanted and settled later, but no one cheated him, and he would be able to tell them what the sisters might fetch on the open market.

The phone rang hesitantly, a jangle rather than a full bell, and Megan said, 'That's playing up. It started just before you got back.' She got to her feet and there was silence round the table, so that Clarry was listening to the wind again.

So were the men. Father and son exchanged anxious looks. 'It's out first light,' said Ralph, and his father nodded. The sheep would have to be accounted for then.

Megan's voice reached them from the phone in the corridor just outside the kitchen door. She was not saying much, but what she did say sounded like bad news. 'Oh, my goodness, I don't like that. Mansell? You there, Mansell?'

She came back. 'That was our Mansell. He says there's trees down, it's a bad night to be on the road.' She was talking to Nicolas. 'Got to get back tonight, have you?'

'You can put us up?' he asked.

'Of course I can.'

He said to Clarry, 'I'll ring through.'

'It went dead,' said Megan. 'I reckon the lines are down.'

'There's a phone in the car,' said Clarry, and to Nicolas, 'Would somebody tell Danny?'

Megan's bright eyes widened and Nicolas said solemnly, 'She has a grandfather who worries about her.'

'They do, don't they, the old folk?' Now Megan's smile was frankly roguish. 'Well, he'll know she's safe enough with you.' As safe as she wants to be, the smile said, obviously enjoying every minute. And for a moment Clarry almost felt guilty about that.

She stood up as Nicolas crossed to the door, with some idea of speaking to Danny herself, but when the heavy old door opened she got the brunt of driving rain and drew back astonished at the wildness out there. Thick walls and the laughter and talk around the table had muffled most of the storm, but nobody would choose to be out on a night like this. There would be accidents. Conditions would be treacherous.

From the doorway she saw Nicolas getting into the car and Megan put a hand on her arm, pointing out, 'No sense getting wet through yourself. Handy things, aren't they, car phones?'

This one was right now, or poor old Danny would have been pacing the floor all night. He wouldn't be thrilled, knowing she was with Nicolas, but he would be relieved to hear that she was safe and staying put.

They left the door open a crack, and Clarry watched through a window. In the light in the car she saw Nicolas talking on the phone, making a brief call, then hurrying back head bent against the wind and the rain.

He came in shaking the rain from him, and told Clarry, 'I spoke to Mrs Haines. She'll tell Danny we'll be back in the morning.'

Pictures flashed through Clarry's mind of how that news would be received at King's Lodge. The face of the housekeeper, turning from the phone, eager to tell whoever was near her, 'That was Mr Dargan. They won't be back tonight. Him and that girl who got soot all over him this morning.'

Danny's face, showing nothing, greeting the information with a grunt. And Fiona Stretton glittering with fury, if anyone was rash enough to tell her. Which somebody would, because nobody liked her much, and Clarry smiled. 'That's all right, then,' she said.

'I'll make up a room,' said Megan, and Clarry squealed,

'*Two* rooms!' Nicolas had just been going to say that. He would have said it quietly and that would have been that, but her shriek made them all smile.

'Separate rooms, of course,' said Megan, eyes dancing. 'Well, there's plenty to choose from if you'd like to come along.'

Only Clarry followed her upstairs, where she opened a door on a room that was adequately furnished. With no luggage Clarry would not be needing the wardrobe nor the chest of drawers, and the mattress looked new and springy, stripped of bedclothes.

She said, 'This will be fine.'

'It's a nice big bed,' said Megan. A generous double, Clarry noted. 'And I'll put Mr Dargan next door.'

Clarry was irritated to find herself blushing, but she could hardly explain that Megan was right off the mark, seeing any connection between a big bed in here and Nicolas Dargan only a few paces away.

All the same, Clarry's cheeks were hot and Megan must be noticing. She looked as if she was, and suddenly she said, 'Of course, you won't have anything, will you, not meaning to stay over, like. Shall I lend you a nightie?'

'That would be kind.' It was cold up here. Her jeans were grubby, she couldn't sleep in them, and her undies were skimpy.

When Megan had gone to fetch some nightwear Clarry began to wonder if she had interpreted that blush as a bashful realisation on Clarry's part that she would be entertaining her lover nearly naked. If he had been her lover it would have been natural and nothing to blush about, but Megan might think a nightdress was more romantic for starters, especially in this icebox of a room where a naked lady could look like a plucked chicken.

She came back with two nightgowns, and one could have been part of a trousseau. It was in the palest of shell pinks, full and frilled and beribboned. Clarry exclaimed, 'This is so pretty!'

Megan held it up, beaming. 'I got it for my honeymoon,' she said.

'Really?' It looked new.

'When Mansell and Jennie got married just a year ago,' Megan explained, 'Bryn and I decided we were due for a honeymoon ourselves. We missed out the first time, you see, got no further than my auntie's in Cardiff, so this time we went to Paris.'

'Really?' said Clarry again.

'Just for the week,' said Megan. 'Lovely, it was, and I bought myself a few pretty things. You'll look lovely in this. I didn't look so bad in it myself.'

'I'm sure you look beautiful in it,' said Clarry.

'That's what my Bryn says,' Megan dimpled, and Clarry thought how sweet it must be to have a man who loved you as a bride after all those years.

The second nightdress had no glamour at all. It was a warm voluminous winceyette, with long sleeves and buttoned up at the back, much more suitable for the kind of night that was ahead for Clarry. She said, 'If you don't mind, I think I'd better take this one. That one's so special, I'd be scared——' she hesitated. Scared of what? Having it ripped off her in a moment of unbridled passion? There was no danger of that, but Megan seemed prepared to take the risk, because she looked thrilled.

'You wear it,' she said, and when Clarry shook her head, 'I tell you what, I'll leave them both.'

'Thank you,' said Clarry, and Megan handed over the nightgowns and went to fetch the bedding.

Clarry helped her make this bed and an identical one in the room next door. Megan obviously thought the second bed was a pure formality, but when it seemed she was going to say something about that Clarry said hastily, 'I've always wanted to go to Paris. Do tell me about it. Where did you stay?' steering Megan into a happy account of her second honeymoon.

Megan pulled the curtains together in both rooms, shutting out the stormy night, and left the light on in the corridor. 'We always let that burn all night when we've got guests staying,' she explained. 'On account of the stairs, you see.'

Halfway down the stairs warmth seemed to wrap around Clarry when voices from the kitchen reached her. Nicolas's voice, deep and amused.

Bryn was telling a tale. He went on with it, but Nicolas looked across at Clarry, and as she settled into her chair beside him he touched her hand as if he was glad to see her back.

They stayed in the kitchen. Megan brought out a bottle of homemade elderberry wine which Clarry thought tasted juicy and rich, probably packing a punch, so she made her glass last. Bryn declined it, 'Never was a wine man,' and produced a whisky which he poured for Nicolas and himself. Ralph and Megan took the elderberry, and it was cosy.

Nicolas listened more than he spoke—he always did, Clarry knew that, but it was his personality that kept the talk going. They might not be aware just how successful he was, but they did know he had charm and class and looked like a good man to have on your side.

He'll have three more fans here after this, Clarry thought, and Megan has lent me her Paris nightgown so that I shall be warm and happy in that big bed upstairs. The jolt of desire that swept through her knocked her dizzy for a moment. The room shivered, but she sat quite still, trying to listen to Megan who was on about tourists who went strolling into the hills in really nasty weather and needed the mountain rescue team to get them down again.

'No sense at all, some folk,' said Megan. 'Wouldn't surprise me if there's not somebody up there now.' There was no let-up in the wind howling round the farmhouse, rattling the door, nor in the sound of rain on the windowpanes.

When the lights went out it should have been no surprise, but Clarry's choked cry was immediate and instinctive. They came on almost at once and she quickly changed her expression, blinking instead of staring wildly. There were no further flickers, the lights stayed steady, and it was Megan who reminded her menfolk that they had to be up early in the morning.

They broke up the party reluctantly, and Clarry was sorry herself to be leaving the warm kitchen. The water was running hotter now, but the bathroom was too cold to strip for a bath. She washed and in the bedroom got into the winceyette nightgown, then jumped into bed, pulling patchwork quilt, blankets and sheets up to her chin. Megan had given her a hot water bottle and said archly and softly, 'I don't suppose you'll be needing this, but take it anyway.'

Clarry had taken it with a twitchy smile and said thank you and goodnight, and now she couldn't make up her mind whether to leave it at her feet or hug it, but one thing was sure, she needed it.

Megan was convinced that Nicolas Dargan was her lover, although surely a man could set out to buy a statue with a woman who was an adviser or an employee, there didn't have to be a personal connection. But Nicolas Dargan had a powerful sexual charisma, and Clarry had not denied anything, and Megan was a romantic.

She wished Megan had been right, but it had been rather a splendid day. She had enjoyed all of it, and now she was tired and huddling herself warm, and the storm was not going to keep her awake.

She left the bedside lamp on and snuggled right down, but she could still hear the wind. There must have been storms in the ironmaster's time, but he would have built his house walls thick with shutters at the windows, and gardeners to repair the damage in the garden. Now the stone sisters were alone in the wind and the rain, and so were the beasts. It must have been a night like this when the griffin was toppled.

Clarry slept heavily at first under the muffling bedclothes, but when she began to dream the wind played its part. It took her up into the garden, and there it was—the cries of the beasts. Not really frightening, just a background chorus to her dream, where she was walking through a misty world of vague shapes.

But suddenly the mist turned black, and she woke into a nightmare of darkness where there was no light and she was as disorientated as if she had fallen into a pit and was still falling. A terror was on her, the mindless panic. She hugged herself, swaying like an autistic child, cold sweat trickling down her body, screaming silently.

Then she heard him, 'Clarry, are you all right?' and her, 'No,' was a whimper, but now there were arms around her and sanity was flowing back into her.

For a little while she couldn't speak at all, and then she could hardly speak for the sobs that choked her. 'I'm sorry—this is so stupid. But I'm afraid of the dark.'

'I know,' he said.

'How do you know?' Her face was pressed against him. She could smell the aftershave or the scent of his skin, and it was like gulping in life. 'Nobody knows.'

'Downstairs when the lights went out, and it made sense of the priest's hole.'

It made no sense to Clarry. Her hair felt cropped and she felt so thin that her bones must be rattling in his arms. She said jerkily, 'Only since the accident. Darkness is like it was then. Darkness is like dying.'

'Clarry,' he said her name very quietly, and she was safe now, answering to her name, coming back but still rigid and aching with tension.

'It's all right, believe me,' he said. He stroked the back of her neck, gently and evenly, undid the buttons and massaged her shoulders, and as the knotted muscles unravelled she gave a little moan of pleasure and relief. I know how a cat feels now, she thought; nobody ever stroked me like this before.

When Nicolas brushed back the hair that was sticking to her forehead she said, trying to smile, 'It's growing again.'

'What is?'

'My hair. Sometimes it feels short and jagged, the way it was. I wasn't unconscious then, just weak and sick, but I can shake my head now——' she let her head fall back so that her hair spilled over his arm '—and it's all right. I do have longish hair, don't I?'

'Long and strong, and a beautiful colour,' he assured her.

'Good, that's a relief.' She was gathering her wits, although it was still an effort to sound rational. 'This is a power failure, isn't it?'

'Yes. The landing light went out too. I'll get you a candle or a lamp.'

That would mean rousing the household. As he moved to stand up she said, 'Don't do that, don't bother them.' He was standing by the bed now, and she put a hand on his arm. 'I've got a torch in my bag somewhere—I always carry a torch. But—

would you stay a little longer?' He hesitated and she said, 'Please,' and he said,

'Of course.' She knew Nicolas was not interpreting this as an invitation to spend the night with her. To him she was a disturbed friend who still needed reassurance, and she was just that, needing someone to talk to, to hold on to for a while although the nightmare was over. She was thinking no further, but she was desperate to keep him here.

She moved along in the bed and he sat down, feet up on the coverlet as he must have done before. She wanted to say something about the chilliness of the room. Although she had been sweating with fear only minutes ago it was cold. She could see now that he was naked to the waist, and he would have been warmer under the quilt at least. But when she had touched him he had not felt cold, and there was no casual way of asking, 'Why don't you get into my bed?'

She said, 'If I didn't panic I'd remember you can see in the dark if you wait.' She could make out the shapes of furniture now and where the window was behind the curtains. She could see him clear and close, and he put an arm around her again as she explained, 'It's sudden darkness that throws me, and sudden and total darkness doesn't often happen, thank goodness. That's why nobody knows about this, not even Danny. Don't tell Danny.'

'Why not?' and she launched fervently into her reasons.

'Because he's gone through enough over me. He was there, every day. He slept by the phone when he wasn't by my bed, and as soon as they let him he took me home with him. I needed nursing, and he paid for everything I needed. And when I started my business he worked with me, although he'd earned his retirement and he could have been taking it easy, and he found the money out of his savings to back me. It's thanks to him that I've got a home and a business, but he is an old man and I don't want him to start worrying if he ought to be getting me to a psychiatrist.'

She was in dead earnest, but Nicolas was smiling. 'What would a psychiatrist do for you that I can't do?' and that made her smile too.

'Let me talk.'

'And what are you doing now?'

Telling more than she would have told anyone else, as if she believed that nobody else could make things as right as this man could. He had pulled her out of the pit tonight. Left alone she would have come round shattered, with that awful fear in her mind that some brain cell somewhere had been damaged and this was a foretaste of madness. She drew a long shaking breath and said, 'It's a crazy way to carry on, isn't it? Am I crazy?'

'You're lucky,' he said. 'You could have been paralysed, you could have been brain-damaged, but you came out of a five weeks' coma with just one small phobia.'

A phobia, that was all it was; a hangover that she would grow out of in time. If it happened again she would not lose control of her mind, she would keep telling herself, I'm not dying, I'm alive and I have everything to live for. I'm lucky.

She said, 'You make a good psychiatrist—I think I'm cured.' They both knew she was not, but from now on there would be a glimmer of light in the darkness.

'You're a good patient,' said Nicolas. 'Anything else?'

'Like what?'

'You told me I owed you.' She had said that outside the maze that first night, for keeping Nigel away from her. 'I do feel some responsibility for your accident,' he said. 'You were riding one of my horses.'

She had thought they were Nigel's horses, not that that mattered, and she quite liked the idea of Nicolas feeling some responsibility for her. She said, 'She was a lovely horse.'

She remembered how the chestnut roan had gleamed in the sunshine, and she was glad, weeks later when she could ask, to learn that the horse wasn't hurt. It had reared when a car backfired, thrown Clarry against a wall, and raced off down a high street, coming to a halt when someone grabbed the trailing reins.

Now she asked, 'Do you still have her?'

'Yes. She's a safer mount now. She wasn't fully trained in traffic when he took you out. You were an inexperienced rider and you shouldn't have been on her.'

She said, smiling, 'He said she matched my hair.'

'It was the only way you were a match for her in those days,' Nicolas said drily.

Clarry could remember nothing of that day beyond the blossom on the cherry trees when they came off the bridle path into the village, but she felt that if Nicolas Dargan had been her companion she would have been safe. 'I wouldn't be a match now,' she said. 'I hadn't done much riding before, and I've never been on a horse since.'

'That's another thing, then.'

'Huh?' she queried.

'You're scared of the dark and you're scared of horses, since the accident. If we deal with them you'll be good as new.' He was joking, and so was she.

'Sure I will. Then I'll only have to dye my white streak and I can forget it ever happened.'

If the horse had not thrown her she might have been with Nigel now, lying somewhere in the darkness beside him with a wedding ring on her finger, which would have been wrong, because she had never wanted Nigel as much as she wanted Nicolas Dargan. She had thought it was love with Nigel. What it was for Nicolas she didn't really know, but she couldn't stop herself turning towards him, the bedclothes slipping from her as her arms reached up and her hands clasped behind his head to draw him against her.

Leaning over her, he looked down. 'What *are* you wearing? Where did you get that?'

She had wanted his mouth on hers, she had wanted him covering all of her, but his smile was like a caress and she could feel the warmth of him inside her so that the closeness was almost a lovemaking.

'Megan lent it to me,' she told him. Even with the buttons undone and one shoulder bared it looked prim and proper. 'I see nobody lent you anything.' She put on a mournful face, although the nightgear of the Thomas menfolk wouldn't have covered the half of it.

'I wasn't offered a water bottle either,' he said. Her bottle was down between the sheets somewhere.

She stretched a leg and wobbled it and suggested, 'They couldn't have thought you needed warming up—Megan certainly didn't.'

'I'd gathered that,' said Nicolas drily. 'The woman's an incurable romantic.'

'Nothing wrong with that, she has the nightdress for it too. She gave me a choice, this and that one over there.' Draped over a chair, the shell-pink nightgown was a shimmer in the shadows. 'She wore that on her honeymoon.'

He was impressed. 'She offered you the heirloom?'

'Sort of. Although this was a second honeymoon, this time last year when Bryn took her to Paris.'

'I hope it was warmer there than it is here!'

Clarry said sweetly, 'It's warmer here, under the bedclothes,' and he laughed.

'I'm sure it is, but that could lead to complications.'

He was not laughing at her, she felt that he never would. 'I don't care,' she said.

'I do. And so would you in the morning. Now, where's that torch?' He got up, but it was not a drawing away, the bond still held between them.

'I don't need it,' said Clarry. 'I can see now.'

Nicolas drew back the curtains so that a grey light filtered through the windows. 'Then get some sleep,' he said, and she could see him clearly. She could have shut her eyes and still seen him.

'Ah, well,' she said, 'I got the griffin.'

'And when you ask Danny Hill to repair the wing you'll be able to look him straight in the eye and assure him it didn't cost you a thing.'

If Danny could see her now he wouldn't know her. 'Because you're handing me back in pristine condition,' she quoted gaily. 'Pure and uncorrupted.'

He laughed again, and so did she as the door closed behind him. Then softly to herself sliding down into the bed, because she knew with a clairvoyant certainty that Nicolas Dargan would be her lover, because in some strange way he already was.

CHAPTER SIX

No, I wouldn't have regretted it in the morning, Clarry thought, waking next morning alone in her bed. The power must still be off. The bedside lamp gave no light and she had to peer closely at her watch to see that the time was a quarter to eight.

The windowpanes were wet but rain no longer lashed them, and the gale-force winds had dropped. When a pale dawn was breaking she had heard voices, doors closing and a dog barking, and had known that the men were going up into the hills searching for the sheep. She had gone to sleep again, but now it was high time she was up and about.

As she moved to push back the bedclothes there was a tap on the door and Megan appeared carrying a tray. 'Cup of tea?' she said brightly. 'Mr Dargan said not to wake you before.'

'He's up, is he?' queried Clarry.

'Been down some time, on that phone of his in the car.' Megan put the tray on the bedside table. 'Power's still off, mind your step on the stairs,' and with another smile and a nod she tripped out again.

Clarry poured herself tea with a splash of milk, and a heaped spoonful of sugar—she was going to need her energy today. She took the cup into the bathroom because if Nicolas was downstairs, making phone calls, he would be ready to leave.

Her reflection in the mirror over the washbasin was wan. The white walls and the chill in the air drained her of colour so that she looked as washed out as the landscape glimpsed through the window. Even her dark red hair seemed duller than usual. She really was very ordinary. She remembered saying to Paul Burnley, 'I'm not conceited enough to go after one his size,' but, however you looked at it, she had propositioned Nicolas Dargan last night and he had turned her down.

This morning her confidence was ebbing away, and she went downstairs not knowing how she was going to face him. She would try to be natural and relaxed, but she could find herself blushing and stammering, and even when her hand was on the latch of the kitchen door she still held back for a few more seconds.

Then she opened the door, and all the warmth of the house seemed to be in the kitchen. An oil lamp burned on the table. Megan Thomas was talking and Nicolas was listening to her, sitting with a cup of coffee before him. Megan stopped talking, and Nicolas smiled at Clarry, and again she had this feeling that he reached out and she homed in to him.

'Sleep well?' he asked.

'Very well, thank you, and you?'

'Of course.' They smiled at each other as she sat down beside him, and Clarry knew that Megan would be smiling too; and Megan was nearly right, for a little while last night they had shared that bed in Clarry's room.

'How about a nice cooked breakfast?' Megan suggested.

The power lines might be down, but the stove gave a good heat and Clarry would have liked to linger, half listening to Megan's prattle, sitting by Nicolas and basking in the warmth of his male sensuality. But she knew that was out of the question, so she said, 'Just tea or coffee for me, please.'

'I can recommend the oatcakes,' he said, and there was a plate of still warm oatcakes on the table with butter and honey. He drained his cup. 'I'm expecting a call, I'll see you out in the car.'

Now Megan poured her a coffee and she buttered herself an oatcake, and swallowed and gulped and said how much she had enjoyed her brief stay.

'Pity you can't make it longer,' said Megan, 'but he's a busy man, isn't he? Big name, Bryn was telling me.'

'Yes,' said Clarry, and a small sigh escaped her before she could check it.

Outside the outlook was miserable. The storm was played out, but there was still a drizzle of rain and the wind kept up a perpetual sighing. Megan looked up to the hills where her menfolk were shepherding their flock, and Clarry looked across at the car where Nicolas was still on the phone.

When they reached the car the griffin was a sinister shape wrapped in sacking, and Megan said, 'I still can't think why you picked him.'

'Picked who?' asked Clarry, pretending not to understand, and for the moment Megan was flustered.

Then Clarry grinned and Megan said, 'Get along, with you, you know I wasn't meaning Mr Dargan.'

Nicolas finished his phone call and leaned across to open the door for her, and Clarry slid into the seat beside him. He thanked Megan, and she said she wished all her guests were as agreeable or anywhere near as generous. By which Clarry reckoned that Megan had been well satisfied when the account was settled, and it had been almost like making new friends.

Megan waved them goodbye, hoping to see them again, but Clarry doubted if Nicolas would be returning or that he ever stayed in a bed-and-breakfast. Perhaps she might come back herself some time. Alone, or with a friend who was not Nicolas Dargan. But if she did she would remember him, and if she woke in the night in one of those bedrooms she would lie there aching to hear him say, 'Clarry, are you all right?'

She would not be all right. She would be missing him so badly that she could never come here again without him. So it was a real goodbye to Megan Thomas who stood at the five-barred gate as long as she could see the car or Clarry could see her.

The farmhouse and the ironmaster's garden could all have been a dream, except for the griffin. He was real and solid, and when she stopped waving at Megan Clarry stretched over to touch the sacking, feeling the rock beneath. 'He's still here,' she said.

'It's unlikely anyone would be out last night hijacking him,' said Nicolas, 'and he wouldn't get far himself on one wing.'

He was joking, and she smiled, but it had been magical for her, although she couldn't expect him to understand.

The first tree down would have soon presented a problem if they had set off last night. It had crashed, uprooted, across the road just below the row of houses. A couple of men were sawing off branches, and going slowly and carefully they managed to get past, but in the darkness, at the height of the storm, that might not have been possible. Even if Mansell Thomas had not made a last phone call they would probably have been turning here and driving back to the farmhouse.

There were signs of storm on the road to the market town, trees and hedges blown all ways, tiles gone from roofs, the chimneystack of one cottage brought down in a tumble of bricks. A mile or so before the town the damage slackened off and there was less evidence of last night, although the town itself was dark; the power cuts had reached here. Illumination in houses and shops was from lamps and generators, and policemen guided traffic where warning lights should have been.

Owen and Davis, the estate agents, were open. Again they parked near and Nicolas left Clarry in the car while he went in. This morning he was back almost before she could sit up and start to look up and down the high street, and from then on they wasted no time.

He drove fast, and the road surface had to be slippery, but she felt he was always in control of the car although obviously intent on getting back to King's Lodge as soon as possible. She was quiet. He was concentrating on the traffic flow, he had done that on the way down, of course, but now he seemed distant and unapproachable.

He turned on the radio, and Clarry felt that was to fill the silence and shut her up. She could have been mistaken, but she could think of nothing to say that mattered much, and Nicolas hardly spoke at all.

When he did he sounded pleasant enough—the name of a town they were passing through, a comment on an item that was being broadcast, but only a few words and then he relapsed into silence, and she dried up, and whatever was on his mind it was certainly not Clarry Rickard.

His hands on the wheel were strong enough to tear the griffin out of the ground. Last night they had been gentle, smoothing her terrors away. She knew how it felt to press her cheek on his bare shoulder and against the rise and fall of his chest. She knew his touch. Close to him physically she would always get that buzz running through her nervous system right to her fingertips. But beneath the surface, under his skin, she hardly knew him at all.

Well before midday they turned into the winding lane that led to King's Lodge, and within a few minutes they were driving through the open gates.

Paul Burnley came hurrying to meet them, and Clarry asked, 'Where are you putting the griffin?'

'In one of the outhouses. Do you want to oversee the removal?'

As the car drew up she said, 'I'd better go and find Danny. He'll be worrying, he'll want to know we're back.'

'So run along and reassure him,' he said, and she felt childish and knew that he was losing patience with her.

Nicolas got out of the car, and Paul Burnley gave him his full attention with never a glance at Clarry. 'Did you get anything?' asked Paul, and Clarry was reminded of the estate agent and his anxious-to-please manner, the half-smile, the way he stayed on his toes as if he was waiting for an order to rush off and deal with it.

She opened her door and climbed out of the car, and neither man looked her way. Paul was hopping around. Nicolas was still, a hand in a jacket pocket. 'It needs repairing,' he said, 'but it should serve its purpose. Get it over to the brewhouse.'

It wouldn't have surprised Clarry to see Paul Burnley try to haul the griffin on to his back and stagger across the courtyard with it. Only he wouldn't be able to lift the broken wing, let alone the rest, and of course that wasn't what Nicolas had meant.

It nearly made her smile, but not quite, and she didn't go round the car to join them because Nicolas still seemed unapproachable. Last night she had lain in his arms, now she couldn't even reach out and touch him, and she no longer had much faith in her flair for making him smile.

Paul Burnley had not been the only one looking out for them. Dolly and Mrs Haines were both by a window in the hall when Clarry entered the house, and she knew they had been gossiping until she was just outside the main door. They were agog with curiosity and they both would have loved to ask her the personal questions which could be more than their jobs were worth.

They both wished her good morning and Mrs Haines played safe with, 'Bad weather down there, was it?'

'Dreadful,' Clarry said. 'Like a hurricane!' They had expected that, they had heard the weather reports. They wondered if any further scrap of information might be coming, such as just where the master and this girl had spent the night, and when Clarry closed the subject by asking, 'Do you know where Danny Hill is?' they both said they had no idea and went off into the kitchen.

This was not the kind of house you could wander around shouting, 'Hey, Danny, I'm back!' Yesterday someone had been taking Danny to a specialist timber merchant, looking for oak that could be used repairing the frame. He could still be searching—the wood would have to be a perfect match to satisfy him. He might not be in the house at all, but Clarry opened a few doors and found him in 'their' little parlour.

He had the photographs of the frame on the table, and he was sketching designs for the missing corner.

She leaned over his shoulder to look at them. 'They're beautiful,' she said. He looked and he was such an old stick-in-the-mud, and yet his work could have an ageless freshness.

He went on shading in a leaf so that it stood out as the carving would do. 'We went to Wales,' Clarry said chattily.

'Huh,' said Danny, who obviously knew that, but he might not have been told about the garden, and that would have fascinated him.

She said, 'There was this old garden up in the mountains. The house is falling down now, and the garden's overgrown and everything's going wild, but there were some statues left in garden, and we were looking for something for the centre of the maze here. There's only a seat there now, and a statue seemed a good idea.'

She paused; he had to be listening, but she was getting no response, so she might as well cut it short. 'Then the storm came up with trees falling across the roads, so we stayed at a farmhouse owned by the man who got the statue down the mountain for us. Him and his sons.'

Danny would be less than interested to hear that Nicolas Dargan had rolled up his sleeves and joined the team. 'Do come and see what we got,' Clarry wheedled. 'It's a surprise, it really is.'

She waited just outside the door until she heard Danny's chair squeak as he stood up and knew that his curiosity was winning. Then she walked ahead, pausing at the top of the stairs until he joined her.

He said nothing and neither did she, but doors were open on what had once been an outhouse for the brewing of ale. Two men who worked on the estate were inside with Nicolas and Paul Burnley, and there was a barrow that had transported the griffin, who now lay on the sacking on a long slabbed sink.

Danny walked over and looked down, and Nicolas asked, 'Can you repair it?'

To Clarry's despair, when Danny raised his head it was to scowl furiously at him. 'Not me,' he said. 'Too big a job for me.'

It should have been no problem, it was well within Danny's range, and nobody could have missed the glare that went with the refusal. This was not a man who was sorry he couldn't oblige; this was a man who was damned if he would. 'If you say so,' Nicolas said curtly, and turned to Paul Burnley, and the two men walked out, going towards the house, discussing something.

In the outhouse the gardeners were getting a closer look at the statue. 'Different, anyway,' said one. 'What is it?'

Clarry said, 'It's a griffin. I know because Danny carved one for me years ago.' She was mad at Danny, but she was still trying to soften him up, telling him, 'I told Nicolas about the one I've got at home, and I was thrilled when we found this one in the garden and he seemed to think it was suitable.'

'Hmm,' said Danny, and Clarry thought, One day you're going to grunt at me and I'm going to scream.

As he stomped off one of the men said, 'Relation of yours, is he?'

'Sort of,' shrugged Clarry.

'Well, he's going the wrong way with Mr Dargan. He won't get asked again. Somebody else'll do this job.'

She knew that, and she could have shaken the stubborn old mule. The statue would have to be cleaned, especially where it had lain in the earth, but left weathered. And the wing would need a metal support. She could do it herself—she wanted it to be set up in the maze before she left King's Lodge.

She stroked the wing for luck and went back to the house, where she intended to spend the next hour taking a warm scented shower, then putting on enough make-up to liven up her looks. Since they had got back here, and for a while before, she had felt like the invisible woman. Nicolas hadn't noticed her, she doubted if he had even seen her.

It was bad luck that as she was going up the stairs she met Fiona Stretton coming down. Meeting Fiona any time was never going to make Clarry's day, but this morning, when Clarry was looking drab and dreary, Fiona looked devastating. Rich and pampered, in a suit that Princess Diana might have worn, with no lock out of place in her cap of smooth hair.

She stopped three steps up, looking down, so that Clarry, who was climbing slowly and holding the handrail, paused too. Fiona smiled, 'I hear you got caught in the storm.'

'Yes,' said Clarry.

'How boring for you.'

'You think so?'

Fiona gave a throaty little laugh. 'Oh, I do. No woman would look like you if she'd just made it with Nicolas. You look more like someone whose hopes came to nothing.'

Clarry yawned. 'I didn't get much sleep last night,' she said. 'Excuse me if I don't stay to chat,' and she walked past Fiona.

The woman was poison, but this time she was not ridiculous, because in a warped and wounding way she had hit on the truth.

Danny was back at the table with his sketches. He would do a superb job on this carving repair and Clarry supposed she should be grateful for that, but he was giving Rickard Restoration a bad name. Nobody was going to recommend such a grudging worker as Danny seemed bent on proving himself.

This wasn't his normal behaviour. He didn't usually glare at folk; most folk liked old Danny. His trouble here was Nicolas Dargan, and before she went up to bathe and change she had to make him understand how stupidly he was acting.

She sat down, facing him, and said, 'Listen to me—I want to do some good work here, and it won't help if you get on the wrong side of Nicolas Dargan every time you meet him. Just now you practically spat at him, and that's cutting our own throats. It's stupid, and it's not fair either. Give him a break, can't you?'

She bit her lip on a wry smile at the thought of Nicolas Dargan needing a break from Danny Hill and went on, 'We were prejudiced, both of us. I really knew nothing about him until we came here, except that Nigel did what Nicolas told him to do, but now I have met him I quite like him.'

'Like' was hardly the word for the confused intensity of her feelings. 'He can be very kind,' she added.

'Kind!' Danny repeated that as if it needed thinking about. Then he said, 'Digging for Dargan's heart would be like hitting granite,' and Clarry's eyebrows shot up.

'That's the nearest to poetry I've ever heard from you!'

'I'm not much for poetry,' said Danny. Nor was he. 'But I remember something about the leopard never changing its spots.'

'I don't think that's quite poetry either,' said Clarry, 'But while we're on the subject of granite-hearted beasts, what about the griffin? Are you going to mend him?'

'I've got this to finish.'

He was still holding the pencil he had been sketching with, and she saw the tremor in the gnarled hands that had always been rock-steady. He *was* old, and this was distressing him, and she said quickly, 'That's all right, I'd like to do it myself.' She reached across the table to take his hand, and her voice and her face softened. 'Only let's forget what happened with Nigel. It was a long time ago and it might have been for the best. I don't want you upsetting yourself.' She grinned. 'I don't want you getting the pair of us chucked out of here either, so let's try to forget it happened. Please.'

'I remember more than you,' Danny said heavily.

Of course he did, she had been ill and two years was a longish while for her, but at Danny's age it might seem like yesterday. '*Please*,' she said again, and he nodded slowly, and that was as near she was going to get to a promise that he would stop antagonising Nicolas Dargon.

'I need a bath,' she said briskly. 'There wasn't much hot water in the farmhouse and then the power went off. I don't think I'll take a shower, I shall take a long soak.'

As she stood up Danny said. 'We've got to get going, you know.'

'Going where?'

'It's Saturday—weekend. We don't work weekends. We go back, see what's going on. Get what we'll be needing for next week.'

She hadn't packed much because she had planned to return home at the end of the week, and it astonished her now that she could have forgotten that. Her world seemed centred on King's Lodge these days, but her home was Danny's bungalow, her business was based in the unit. There would be matters there to be attended to and she needed changes of clothing. She had only brought working clothes and she would like at least one decent outfit.

Not that she was competing with Fiona Stretton, she had nothing that would compare with anything the golden girl wore, but Nicolas had never seen her looking remotely glamorous, and maybe it was time that he did.

But she couldn't be away from here for a whole weekend, so she said, 'We could go tomorrow, we can do that easily there and back and have time to deal with whatever's waiting. There shouldn't be much. Lucy and the answerphone have kept us up to date. Besides, there's more work now, there's the griffin.'

Danny was going to protest, his mouth was opening. 'And,' she went on, 'the less time we waste the sooner we finish.'

He shut his mouth at that and picked up his pencil again. 'Did you get the wood?' she asked. He nodded. 'Good,' she said. 'That's very good. Matching old oak like that could have been tricky.' Danny might not be happy, but he was working on something he enjoyed and now perhaps she could have her bath.

She opened the door and almost fell over the girl who was about to walk in and who said, 'Phone call for you, miss,' and gave her the same bright-eyed inquisitive look Clarry had encountered when she was about to have lunch with Nicolas that first day and this girl was laying a table.

Since then there had been the night away together, and here was one who did not share Fiona's conviction that Clarry's hopes had come to nothing. 'Thank you,' said Clarry, and went quickly towards the nearest phone before she started blushing.

She had had several phone calls here and expected a familiar voice, but the soft Welsh lilt was unexpected. 'This is Megan Thomas, Miss Rickard. I'm ringing you from a friend's—our lines are still down, but I did want a word with you and ask you to thank Mr Dargan for me. Bryn says he's a busy man and I shouldn't be disturbing him phoning, that I should be writing a letter, but I thought you wouldn't mind, and I didn't want to wait. I'm so pleased, it was such a surprise!'

'What was?' asked Clarry when she could get a word in.

'You didn't know? Well, that was nice of him too, not making a show of it, but he told Mr Owen that I was to have the choice of the girls in the garden.'

To Nicolas Dargan it would be like buying someone a box of liquorice allsorts, but it had been a nice gesture, and Megan was delighted.

'I'm glad one of them's sure of a good home,' said Clarry.

'I know just where I shall put her on the patio,' Megan said happily, 'and I know which one I want. There's the one with her nose chipped—she's been like that for years, I used to feel sorry for her, but now I think she's the pretty one and she's the one I like.'

'I saw her,' said Clarry. 'I liked her best.'

'And you'll thank him for me? He really is a lovely man!'

'I'm beginning to think he is,' Clarry agreed.

So now she had a message to deliver. She had to find Nicolas and say, 'Megan Thomas phoned. She asked me to thank you and say she's always wanted the one with the broken nose.' That shouldn't interrupt him too much if he was busy, and if Fiona was with him it would give her something to wonder about.

He could still be with Paul Burnley, they could be in the agent's office, they could be anywhere, but the office off the King's Room was on this floor, and Clarry went there first. The inner door was open and he sat at the desk, reading a page in a sheaf of papers. When Clarry reached the doorway he looked up. 'Be right with you,' he said.

She stayed where she could see him, and when he put down the page and looked up again she said, 'Sorry to interrupt, but there was a call from Megan Thomas.'

'You're not interrupting, I was coming for you as soon as I got through here.'

There was what looked like a lot of work on the desk, but hearing him say that he would be with her when his time was free sent her spirits soaring. She could still make him smile, he was smiling now, and she said, 'Bryn said not to disturb you, but Megan couldn't wait to say thank you for fixing it for her to get a free statue, and she wants me to tell you that.'

'I never did find out what Bryn thought of them,' he said. 'He might not be thanking me.'

'He'll be glad she didn't want a griffin outside the window. She wants the nymph with the broken nose. She likes broken noses.'

'A woman with taste,' Nicolas remarked.

'And she thinks you're a lovely man.'

'Her judgement's not so sound there.'

She nearly admitted she had agreed with Megan, but decided against it. Instead she said, 'I can mend the griffin's wing.'

'Fine.'

'Danny is——'

'I know what Daniel Hill is,' Nicolas said grimly. 'He's a good craftsman, and that's why he's here. He's also a bloody old fool, and I don't suffer fools gladly, so keep him out of my way.'

Hot words trembled on her lips and her body went rigid. She wanted to leap to Danny's defence, but he *had* been behaving badly, and Nicolas

Dargan was not a patient man, much less a lovely man right now.

She said coldly, 'I have talked to him, and I don't think you'll have any more trouble.'

'Right. Now,' he gestured towards the desk and the papers on it, 'I'll need another hour or so on this; will you meet me here afterwards?'

'Discussing business?'

'No.' He seemed to have put the problem of Danny out of his mind. 'Shall we say one o'clock?'

He was waiting for her reply, although the last time he got no for an answer must have been long ago. After a moment she shrugged and said, 'Why not? I'm not likely to get a better offer.'

She was disappointed and she was riled. She had told Nicolas how much she owed to Danny and, knowing that, she had flattered herself that he would make allowances for the old man. But he didn't 'suffer fools', and she should have been prepared for that; there weren't many tolerant tycoons about. From now on she must remember how tough and uncompromising he was, and she must talk less about Danny—she had tended to go on about him—and keep him away from Nicolas Dargan.

Life might be simpler if she kept out of his way herself, but she no longer had a choice there, because although he was harder than nails there was nobody she would rather be with.

She had her warm scented bath and she changed into her last pair of clean jeans and a polo-neck Aran sweater. She brushed her hair until it shone, and she creamed her face and brightened eyes, cheekbones and lips, then sat for a while, elbows on the dressing-table, fingers laced under her chin, killing time like someone waiting for a show to start.

What they would do this afternoon she had no idea. She was walking into a bedroom, but she would have the surprise of her life if she ended up on the King's bed. Last night, in the storm and the darkness, it had seemed that Nicolas Dargan was her secret lover, but she couldn't see him seducing her in broad daylight, under the same roof as Danny and Fiona and the rest of them.

She hugged herself at the thought. As a thought it was better than any novel, and she daydreamed a little, but it was not going to happen, although just being with him made life brighter and sharper as if danger was never far away.

She was not losing her head over the man. He must like her, but there must be so many other women who could take her place. He could replace her, no trouble. Fiona Stretton was nearer his match and she hadn't managed any kind of commitment.

Clarry knew all that, but when she walked into the King's Room, and Nicolas came out of the office to meet her, her heart began racing as if she had been running in a marathon and her knees went weak. I may be keeping my head, she reflected ruefully, but he's having an extraordinary effect on the rest of me!

'It's stopped raining,' she said tritely. It had stopped before they got back, and she chattered on, 'When would you like me to start on the griffin?'

'Certainly not now.'

'What are we doing now?'

'I thought we might start your rehabilitation,' said Nicolas.

'My *what*?'

'Facing the phobias.'

'You are joking?' She started to laugh. 'How? Don't tell me you're putting me back in the priest's hole and I won't feel a thing this time?' Of course he was joking. 'Maybe I wouldn't, I'd be ready for the lid closing, but I really do not fancy that.'

'That wasn't the idea,' he said, 'although our safe place was considered a model. Charles said it was one of the best he'd come across, and he knew his hides. At that time his loyal subjects were shoving him into them the length and breadth of the country.'

Clarry pulled a face and gave an exaggerated shrug. 'So it had the royal seal of approval, but nobody's getting me in there again.'

'So we'll start on the horses.'

She had not been on a horse since the accident, but that was not because she had been left with a fear of them. It was not as if she had seen the animal rearing over her or been dragged along screaming. The last thing she remembered everything had been fine, and if Nicolas Dargan was taking her riding she was willing to go. She knew she would be safe with him. 'Shall we go round the Shire Horse Centre?' he was asking her, and she said,

'I'll go anywhere.'

'I'll remember that.'

'I'll get my coat.'

She went to fetch her duffel coat and looked into the parlour where Danny was eating his lunch. There was food on the table and a place laid for her, but eating would have to wait. She took a bread roll, buttered it and slapped in a slice of chicken. 'I'm going to see the Shire Horse Centre,' she mumbled, getting the roll down as quickly as she could and hoping she would not get violent indigestion.

Danny nodded, and that was all she told him. Then it was back into the car, with Nicolas at the wheel again, and although she didn't look back at the house she knew they were being watched from more than one window.

The Centre was only a few minutes away from the Manor House by car. It had been a dairy farm on the edge of the village, now it was a stud farm, a nature trail and a farm park, with the shire horses as the main attraction.

They drove down the wide track, past the old farmhouse, a restaurant and a gift and tackle shop, into the car park, joining a smattering of cars. Weekend visitors. This was a wintry day, the summer months must be their best time.

As they walked towards buildings an open wagon passed, with half a dozen passengers muffled up against the cold, off on a guided tour by the man holding the reins, and with a very large horse between the shafts.

The driver flicked a long whip in salute. 'Afternoon, Mr Dargan,' and Nicolas signalled back.

'Good afternoon.'

'He doesn't use that thing, does he?' muttered Clarry.

'The whip? Not on Drummer. He's a gentle giant.'

Passing by her, the shire horse seemed enormous, must weigh a ton, and when they walked into the stables a row of huge heads, looking over the doors, loomed above her. There was a notice—'These Horses May Bite'—and with teeth that size you would have to be mad to touch them.

But Nicolas did, stroking them, using their names, Trooper and Duchess, and Clarry thought, You're a giant of a man, so maybe that evens things out, as a girl came hurrying down the central passageway, in khaki sweater and cords and green wellies, smiling broadly. 'Oh, Mr Dargan, I thought I heard your voice.'

Dargan Enterprises were backing this family enterprise, but Clarry could see that the girl was smitten by the man. She was young and pretty and she would have liked to touch him. Her fluttering fingers stopped just short of his arm, and the look she gave Clarry when he introduced them was frankly envious.

She chattered breathlessly, rather as I do at times, Clarry thought. He can take your breath away. Business wasn't bad at all, she said, and they had some special events planned over Christmas. Perhaps Mr Dargan might get along to some of them or the New Year's Eve party.

She said that wistfully, and he was charming and non-committal, promising nothing, and Clarry felt rather sorry for her, but she was obviously thrilled to have him here now. There was a booking tonight, she said, the Young Farmers were having a buffet supper and a barn dance; and the stables opened into an arena large enough for a horse show, with straw in squared bales stacked in seating tiers round the walls.

At the far end a man was braiding the tail of a horse and the girl called, 'Dad, it's Mr Dargan,' at which the man beamed a welcome too and began to tell Nicolas how they were making out, as though this might be an inspection tour.

Clarry didn't think it was, although she supposed Nicolas could be checking on his investment, and she couldn't take her eyes off the horse.

The more she saw of the shires, the more impressive they seemed to get. This one was gleaming black, with a white star on its forehead, towering above Clarry, a massively powerful animal.

'What do you think of Humphrey?' Nicolas was asking her.

Humphrey looked down his long nose at her, his dark liquid eyes shining. 'He's magnificent.' She stroked the muscular neck. 'He's gorgeous!'

'You're not nervous with him?'

'No,' she smiled.

'Are you up to riding again?'

She hopped well back at that. 'Oh, my gosh, you're not getting me up on one his size!'

They all chuckled. Nicolas said, 'They carried knights in armour once, but they've been haulage animals since armour went out of fashion. If the oil ever runs out they'll be in big demand again. No, we'll find you one nearer the ground.'

The girl took over braiding Humphrey's tail and her father went with them to other stables, in a yard behind the farmhouse. The horse they brought out for Nicolas was a bay hunter, handsome and haughty, snorting and pawing the ground, and Clarry was glad he was not for her.

They brought her a grey mare, plumper and steadier, and Nicolas insisted she wear a hard hat, and held the reins while she put her foot in the stirrup and hauled herself astride. She was a novice, that morning with Nigel he had been only her second time in the saddle, but she had been managing well enough so far as she remembered, and this seemed a docile mount, not too far off the ground.

She settled into the rhythm as they trotted out of the yard, crossing a field and passing an ornamental lake where farmyard white ducks and turquoise-feathered wild mallards swam together. In summer tourists would be picnicking on the banks, but today there was no one around and the two horses plodded on.

Nicolas was holding the hunter back, and when Clarry gave the grey her head she began to trot. 'All right?' Nicolas asked.

'*Yes*.'

She surely was. She could not remember a time when things had been more brilliantly right. She felt a surge of confidence, as if she had won a gold medal and was mounting a rostrum, a winner who knows that the gods love her. Her horse went from a trot to a canter and she wanted the wind through her hair. 'Can I take off my hat?' she asked.

'No, you may not.' But he was laughing with her, and now they were galloping, and Clarry was so high that if they had come to a five-barred gate she might have believed she could jump it. If she had she would have gone over alone, because the grey was not built for jumping anything, and after a few minutes at full stretch the mare slackened her pace and they were back to a canter.

'You're a natural,' Nicolas told her.

'Am I?' His praise made her glow, it *was* the gold medal, something to treasure. With anyone else she would have ridden competently, but with him it was as if there were no limits to what she could do. She couldn't explain it, she just *knew*.

He checked his watch. 'We should be getting back.' She would have liked to ride on, but he was turning towards the Centre again and they reached the stables, where a groom came out to meet them.

Nicolas handed the reins of his horse over and helped Clarry dismount, and as she slid down she said, 'Another phobia dealt with—that was lovely!'

She had been cheating, letting him think she was nervous about riding, but she was certainly nervous now in his arms, stretching up, looking up, so that he only had to bend a little to touch her lips.

That was unlikely, in front of the groom and who knew how many more, and words ran through her mind... I've never wanted to make love with any man since Nigel jilted me. Is that another hangover from the accident? Could you help me there?

But she could never say that, and he loosed her as soon as she was steady on her feet, and ten minutes later they were in the car driving back to King's Lodge. On the way Nicolas said, 'I have to be in London this evening. Will you come with me?'

She was unprepared for that. She gasped, 'Leaving right now?'

'In about half an hour.'

Dreaming was fine, she could control dreams, but this panicked her so that she was stammering, 'I have to go home and collect things I shall need here. And business mail—I do have a business to run.'

'Another time, then? Maybe next weekend?' That was not a business offer, but he could hardly have sounded more casual if it had been, and when she couldn't get her voice working he said, 'Think about it.'

She managed, 'I will, I'll think about it.' Outside the house she said, 'Goodbye for now, thanks for everything,' and scrambled out and walked ahead, not seeing or hearing anybody as she climbed the stairs and reached the little parlour.

Danny was snoozing, in an armchair in front of the fire, and she sat down and thought about it.

She had been propositioned. Nicolas Dargan had admitted he wanted her, and she wanted him so much that it terrified her. If he had followed it up she would have been a pushover, her defences were so fragile when she was near him that it was hard to think clearly. But she knew that in the long run an affair with him could cause her more pain than she could bear.

Away from him, and away from here, she might be able to weigh the pros and cons with a cooler mind, and if Nicolas Dargan was not in King's Lodge her reason for staying had gone. She admitted that to herself and said, 'Danny,' leaning forward and waiting for Danny's eyelids to flutter.

When he seemed more or less awake she said, 'It isn't late, we could get home early evening if we leave now. What do you think?'

Danny got up. 'I'm ready,' he said.

It was dark well before they stopped, first at the trading estate where Clarry collected her mail from the unit, and then parking the van in the garage beside the bungalow. She turned on the house heating and fetched fish and chips for supper. In the shop they asked, 'How's it going?' and she said, 'Fine, it's a fabulous old house,' and wondered what the servers and the customers would think if she told them, 'I'm going crazy for the multimillionaire who owns it, and Danny hates his guts.'

Back in his own home Danny was in a mellower mood. He ate his supper and watched television and chuckled over a comedy series, while Clarry sat at the living-room table dealing with Rickard Restoration matters.

She rang the girl who had been going into the unit each day and keeping her posted at King's Lodge, and they chatted like the friends they had become since they found themselves neighbours on the trading estate a year ago, but Clarry never mentioned Nicolas. And when Lucy suggested Clarry joined her and a few others in a Saturday night fling at a nightclub she pleaded that she was dead beat and had to be away again early tomorrow.

She gave the same excuse to a man who rang, who was one of her dates, and when he asked if she would be home next weekend she said, 'I'm not sure, I may be working.'

She was telling herself then that she did not know how she would be spending next weekend. She was being sensible. She waited until it was late and she was in bed and the house was quiet and there were no distractions, then she tried to consider her problem in a calm and reasonable way.

She was no glutton for punishment, and beyond next weekend there might be nothing. She could be a one-night or two-night stand for Nicolas Dargan, and what would that do for her pride? He had given her no reason to imagine she was more than a brief diversion. A few days ago he had never set eyes on her and a few weeks hence he could have forgotten she existed. The way things were between them now was good, almost fantastic. If they went on like this she could still be in one piece, still her own woman, when they parted.

Letting him make love to her could be madness, but it was no longer a fantasy, and her reasoning went haywire as anticipation coursed through her, sending her blood singing, loosing fountains of delight.

'If you fly you can fall,' he had said, looking at the griffin's broken wing. If I fly I *will* fall, Clarry thought. Soar and burn and come down like a spent rocket, but the soaring and burning will be glorious, and it seemed she had known this for a long time.

Of course she would go with him. She had no pride where he was concerned. She would have gone today if he had given her a chance to get her breath before he said, 'Another time?' And what was the use of trying to listen to the small warning voice in her mind when every other nerve in her body was going wild with joy?

Danny was quiet next morning, but Danny was always quiet, and Clarry did all the things she had to do. While he finished the lunch she had prepared she collected the materials and equipment for repairing the griffin from the unit; then another fifteen minutes clearing up here and everything was loaded into the van but Danny.

He was still pottering around, and she said, 'Come on. I'd rather get there before dark.'

'I'd rather not get there at all,' said Danny.

'You mean not go back?' That was a lunatic idea. 'We've got to. We've taken on the work and we've got to finish it.'

'Might well be the finish, girl,' muttered Danny, and her mouth fell open.

'What are you *talking* about?' He looked shrunken, without hope, and she said incredulously, 'You're not frightened of Nicolas Dargan, are you?'

'No.'

'Did you know something about him I don't know?'

'No,' he said again, and met her puzzled eyes unblinkingly, but for the life of her she couldn't tell if he was lying.

After that he got into the van and they set off. Danny had never been possessive before. If friends suited Clarry they suited him, and he wanted her to find the right man and get married, but he seemed to loathe everything about Nicolas Dargan.

If he knew she was rushing into an affair there it would probably give him a heart attack, so she would try to keep it from him, spinning a story for next weekend. It might be a hole-and-corner arrangement anyway, Nicolas might not want other folk knowing. But whatever happened, whatever the cost, she was going.

The journey went smoothly with no delays. When they reached King's Lodge Clarry parked the van out of the way against the wall and got out carrying her case. Danny was trundling his smaller case, and as they went into the hall the housekeeper hurried out of the kitchen. Mrs Haines had been intrigued after Clarry's last night away from here, but this time she seemed bewildered.

'Miss Rickard,' her voice was strained, and when Clarry turned, 'Mr Dargan said, as soon as you got back, he wants to see you.'

Clarry heard Danny snort and asked, 'Where is he?'

'In the drawing-room, but—Miss Rickard——' Mrs Haines's raised voice trailed away as Clarry dropped her case and went quickly, with long strides, before Danny could attempt to stop her or move to go with her.

Something was wrong. She was almost running along the corridor. In the drawing-room the TV was on and the man sitting in front got up from a high-backed armchair.

'I've missed you,' he said, and although she was speechless with surprise she thought what a hypocritical thing that was for Nigel Dargan to be saying.

CHAPTER SEVEN

'You haven't changed,' said Nigel, and that nearly made Clarry laugh. Maybe the white streak in her hair was the only outward sign, but in every inner way she had changed out of recognition.

'Whatever gives you that idea?' she asked.

His good looks would always be boyish. Compared to Nicolas he would always be immature, and his smile now was unsure, as well it might be.

'It's good to see you,' he said. 'I've just heard you were here.' Behind him the television audience broke into applause and Clarry, shocked to the edge of hysterical giggles, thought, Take a bow, you're putting on quite a show!

He turned the set off. 'Nicolas isn't here?'

'No.' She bet he had heard that too. 'Did you come to see me?' He nodded a yes. 'So what do you want?'

'I wanted to see you. How have you been?'

'Fine. Happy and healthy, and business is building up.' They sounded like casual acquaintances meeting again, and that was how she felt now the shock was wearing off—not particularly interested, just making small talk.

'Shall we sit down?' Nigel was standing by the television. She had not moved from the open doorway, but now she came into the room and closed the door. It would be ridiculous to leave the door open as though it was a way of escape. Then she took a chair and he sat down again in the wingback.

'How are *you*?' She asked the obvious question, and his smile was wry.

'If we're talking about Dargan Enterprises, everybody knows they go from strength to strength.' Everyone who read the financial pages or even the news stories knew that Nigel Dargan must be making a comfortable living. 'But personally,' he said heavily, 'things aren't so good. My marriage is on the rocks.'

'I'm sorry,' she murmured. She did not want to hear this. It was none of her business.

'I should never have listened to Cole.' Nor did she want to listen to that. 'How are you getting on with him?'

Nigel was watching her closely and she said, 'All right,' and hoped her voice was not giving her away. 'We went riding yesterday.'

'He doesn't have his horses here. They're still at the Rawnsley Stables.'

'We were at the Shire Horse Centre.' Nigel gave a jeering snort of laughter.

'But of course, everyone falls over themselves to provide for Nicolas Dargan. How about you?' His eyes narrowed. 'What are you providing?'

'Didn't you hear that too? I'm Rickard Restoration; we restore chimneyplaces, that sort of thing.' But colour was creeping into her cheeks, and Nigel sneered:

'So he's got you too, has he, as well as the live-in lady?' Now the hot blush could pass for anger, and anger was one of the emotions churning in her. 'I should have thought Fiona Stretton would have been enough in the home comforts line. What's he running here, a harem?'

She was saying nothing to that, but she looked at him with such distaste that he tried to justify himself. 'I could be on the wrong track, but Cole knows how things are between Caroline and me. He doesn't want that partnership cracking up, he's got business dealings with Caro's father. And he's guessed I was missing you—he misses nothing, I sometimes think he's a mind-reader. Well, it's a coincidence, isn't it, that he comes down here when you're here, and you're getting on with him, riding with him? How far has he got with you in a week?'

How far? She could have been away with Nicolas now. Burning her bridges, flying and burning. That was how far he had got.

And this explanation made more sense than Paul Burnley's deciding Nicolas was using her to hold off Fiona. Nobody seemed to think that Clarry had what it took to make Nicolas Dargan want her for herself. Come to that, neither did she. Later there might be pain, but now there was only emptiness, which was why she could change the subject as if it bored her, asking, 'How long are you staying?'

Her composure took him aback. 'A few days,' he said, 'unless I'm shown the door. Do you know how long Cole's away for?'

'No.' Clarry got up, and he tried to grin.

'How's old Danny these days?'

'Still chiselling away.' Danny had not disliked Nigel. At least, he never glared at Nigel with the malevolence he showed towards Nicolas Dargan.

As she opened the door Nigel asked, 'You'll come down for dinner?'

'Sure.' She said with a spurious gaiety, 'Get Fiona and the Colonel down too—I've never seen the Colonel. Let's have a party.'

As she walked through the door he said, 'Now you've seen Cole, what chance do you think I had of standing up to him?'

Clarry had asked herself that question more than once, and she answered it for him. 'No chance at all.' She had stopped blaming Nigel ages ago. She had stopped caring about Nigel. She had to stop caring about anything for now.

Danny was waiting for her in the parlour, and she told him, 'That was Nigel.'

'So she said.' The housekeeper had probably been stammering that out while Clarry was hurrying out of earshot.

'His marriage is on the rocks; he's been missing me.' Danny grunted, and she went on, 'He says Nicolas is putting on the charm to keep me away from him—what do you think?'

'Keep away from both of them,' said Danny.

'You don't think I should give Nigel a second chance?' What rubbish she was talking! She could never take up with Nigel again.

'Better him than his cousin,' said Danny. 'Nigel Dargan's not much of a man, but Nicolas Dargan could break you.'

Not while I feel like this, Clarry thought; you can't break nothing. She said, 'I said we'd have dinner downstairs.'

'Not me,' he shrugged.

'Well, I hope it's not going to be just the two of us, because if Nigel wants to tell me again how he picked the wrong girl I shall probably start screaming with laughter.'

Screaming, anyway. She wished she had listened to Danny and they had not come back. She wished she had said just now, 'It's a big house, keep out of our room.'

Staying cool was hard, but that was how she had played it and how she must go on, and it left less time for thinking. When she had changed her travelling clothes for one of the snazzy dresses she had brought back with her, and fixed her face and hair, it was time to go downstairs. She was not dressing up for Nigel, just putting on a good face to hide how wretched she was feeling. And if Fiona was there, the live-in lady, that was another good reason for going down with flying colours.

Her dress was a flame-coloured crêpe shift, with thin straps over smooth bare shoulders. She had thought she might wear it next weekend. Only now there would be no next weekend, because nothing could blot out the suspicion that she was only with Nicolas to prevent her being with Nigel, putting the final strain on a marriage that was good for business if for nothing else.

Fiona had joined them. She was sitting at the table, and she stared when she saw Clarry, with her hair piled artfully, vivid in her red dress, eyes glittering and colour on her cheekbones to hide her pallor.

Nigel said huskily, 'You're as beautiful as ever.'

Clarry smiled, 'So I get told.' She sat down. 'This is Nigel Dargan,' she said to Fiona, 'another old friend of mine, but you must have met.'

They didn't say when, but they agreed that they had, and it was almost like friends dining together. The food was excellent—Clarry appreciated that. She could see how attractive and appetising it looked, although it had no flavour in her mouth. And the wine slipped smoothly and tastelessly down.

Fiona was being a sweetie, she and Nigel had plenty in common, and Clarry could be bright and funny, and tonight she was both. The wine helped, but it was all superficial. Nigel's charm, and Fiona's, seemed skin-deep, but they were young and good-looking and they talked animatedly, and Clarry could have been enjoying herself.

She was looking as if she was, leaning back in her chair smiling, when the door opened and Nicolas walked in.

Nigel yelped, sending his wine splashing red on the white damask cloth. Fiona exclaimed, 'Nicolas!' and started to get up from her chair. Then she sat down again hurriedly, and Clarry thought, He'll push past anyone who gets in his way.

She could feel the anger radiating from him, and they could all hear it when he towered over Nigel, demanding, 'What the hell are you doing here?' His voice was steely and more threatening than if he had shouted.

Nigel gulped, 'We weren't expecting you.'

'I can see that.' Nicolas looked at Clarry and his glare shrivelled her. 'Excuse us,' he said, and to Nigel, 'Let's talk.'

Nigel got up to follow him out of the room, grinning sheepishly at the girls and murmuring, 'Keep the coffee warm!'

Then they were left alone at the table with the spreading scarlet stain of wine between them, and Fiona gasped, 'What was that all about?' Clarry knew, but she was not discussing it, and suddenly Fiona giggled. 'I wonder what young Nigel's been up to. You knew them both before you came here, didn't you?'

'Not well,' said Clarry. 'I knew neither of them well.'

Fiona looked pleased to hear it. She was a little high on the wine, while Clarry herself had suddenly become cold sober. 'Nicolas was terrifying, wasn't he?' said Fiona dreamily. 'I love masterful men.'

'You're welcome to them,' said Clarry. 'Let's talk—hah! Nicolas'll be the only one doing the talking, and whatever he had to say could have waited a few minutes. He didn't need to make it so humiliating. He should have been wearing jackboots!'

Fiona giggled again. 'He *was* angry—I've never seen him like that before.'

'Oh, I'd say it was in character,' said Clarry. 'Perhaps you've never crossed him,' and Fiona gave a little erotic wriggle.

'I've never wanted to.' And she poured herself more wine, smiling her smug smile.

After a silence Clarry asked, 'Where's your father? Isn't he living here too?' Fiona seemed to be enjoying her thoughts, but Clarry was not.

'We have an apartment,' said Fiona. 'He comes and goes,' and that was the end of that.

So am I going, thought Clarry. This is a Dargan affair and I don't even want to be an onlooker. She really felt sorry for Nigel, who could have stood no chance against Nicolas from the day he was born. That man, bulldozing everything in his way, was the real Nicolas Dargan. She did not know him well, but well enough to know that, and she couldn't sit here any longer, waiting and feeling sicker by the minute.

As she got up from the table Nigel came back into the room. 'Sorry about that,' he said. 'I should have been nursing a deal that Cole is determined shouldn't go down the drain. I came here for a break, now I'm back on duty tomorrow.'

The double-talk was for Fiona's benefit, the deal was his marriage, and it was all pathetic. Clarry said, 'You shouldn't have come.'

'I guess not.' He looked very shaken. 'I didn't think he'd be here, and I never thought he'd cut up this rough. He's still out there. He told me to get out of his sight—I don't think he could trust himself near me. I thought he was going to knock me down.' He sat down groggily. 'You'd better keep out of his way too. He's in a bloody murderous mood.'

'That's his problem,' Clarry said airily. 'Goodnight, all.'

She had no strength for any more play-acting. She got out of the room and reached the staircase with her head high although there was no one to see. But she needed the rail to help her up the stairs, and she stopped for a moment by one casement window, looking blindly into the darkened garden.

It was not quite dark out there. Lights from the house reached to where Nicolas was walking the lawn. She was not looking for him, at least she didn't think she was, and it had to be chance that he looked up as if the pale shimmer of her face had caught his attention.

He could get away with murder. Everybody took it from him, whatever he laid on them. Nigel was hopeless. Fiona never crossed him. In business and private life his word was law, nobody stood up against him, and she would probably be out of here tomorrow, but tonight, first, she was going to tell him some home truths.

She tore down the stairs, and was out of the door and haring across the lawn as if the house was on fire. He was still there, further into the shadows, but she could see him plainly, and he heard her coming and turned and growled, 'Well?' when she was near enough to hear.

She took a few more steps before she stopped, and then she said, 'Not very well, no.' She had words ready in her head, and they came in a rush. 'I suppose Nigel's used to it, you must have been treating him like this for ever, but I'm not, and watching you just now knocked me out. So you were mad at finding him here and you don't want his marriage breaking up, but you treated him appallingly. Whistle and he comes to heel—that's it, isn't it? Like a dog. We make a good pair there. He's the dog you crack the whip at and I've been the one you pat on the head. Pet the poodle and the silly bitch will jump through hoops for you.'

Her tongue was running away with her, she was beginning to shock herself when she had to draw breath.

'Have you done?' Nicolas demanded.

'I've done,' she said. 'I don't know what I'm doing out here.'

'You're making a fool of yourself.' He was a stone man, but he was right there.

'Not for the first time,' Clarry said raggedly, 'but it will be the last. We all know how you feel about fools, and I'm pretty sick with myself for being so stupid.'

'Get inside,' he said wearily. 'You're half naked and you'll catch cold.'

Get out of my sight, he had said to Nigel, who had thought he was about to be knocked down. She was in no danger of that, but he was making her feel like a screeching child, and she was not half naked. This was a perfectly respectable dress, although a strap had slipped off her shoulder. She yanked it up so hard the stitches snapped. It was only a bootlace wide, so up or down didn't make much difference, but a trailing strap looked ridiculous, and as Nicolas strode away she found herself dancing on the spot in impotent fury.

No way had that hysterical outburst helped. She had said her say and he couldn't have cared less, and she felt worse for it, not better.

This time she went upstairs breathing slowly and deeply, clutching her shoulder strap and trying to hold herself together emotionally as well. It was not late yet. When she was sure she was in full control she went to the parlour, where Danny was sitting with a book by the fire.

As he looked up she gave him an impish grin. 'I bet it was more exciting down there than in that book! We've just had a very high-powered scene.'

Danny's grizzled eyebrows shot up over the rims of his glasses, and Clarry sat down at the table and laughed, holding the snapped strap. 'This just popped while I was flinging my arms around—it wasn't a fight exactly but pretty near. Nicolas turned up, and he was furious finding Nigel here, looking cosy with me. Absolutely foul! He carried on as though he'd caught us pinching the family silver!'

She was still laughing, although it was getting harder, and she gave up trying to speak and tried to keep smiling until the tears that had welled in her eyes were rolling down her cheeks. She gave up then, burying her face in her hands, because there was no hiding this from anyone. Least of all from herself.

She was not a weeping woman. She must have shed tears sometimes since, but this torrent of grief was how it was after the motorway pile-up when her parents died. Danny had loved them both, since then he had loved and cherished her, and when she looked up now he was sitting opposite her, the deep lines in his face like a carved mask of despair.

'Is it Nigel?' he asked gently, and she shook her head. 'So it is Nicolas.' He sounded as if he had always known that.

So had she. As though there was a bond between herself and Nicolas Dargan so powerful that nothing should have broken it. But it was broken, and now she was alone and adrift and she would never be safe or happy again.

There was no explanation, but she searched for one, stammering, 'It was a sort of obsession. You know it was before we came here, but after I met him it hit me all ways. I hated him and—well, I didn't hate him. Sometimes—like when he first held my hand—it seemed that I should be holding on to him. It was weird. I didn't want to, I wanted to run, but somehow he seemed like a lifeline.'

It could make no sense to Danny, and when he said, 'He didn't tell you?'

Clarry was baffled. 'Tell me what?' she queried.

'I thought he had when I saw the stone griffin. Yours was by your bed in the hospital. Then you said you'd told him about it.'

'What are you talking about?'

'He held your hand when you were in the coma,' Danny told her.

That had to mean he had come to see her. 'Nicolas?' she stammered. 'Not Nigel?'

'Nigel came once, twice, no more. After that, Nicolas came.'

She would not have known, and no one had told her. 'What happened?' she asked.

'I said, "You're the wrong Dargan." He looked at me, he looked at you, and he said, "We'll get her back."'

'And?'

'He got you back. He came most nights.'

This was incredible. It would have made a news paragraph in any paper. Someone would have leaked something like that. She said, 'He must have been seen, why didn't it get talked about?'

'Those who knew kept it quiet. He came quietly, and he's a mighty powerful man.'

Danny would know, Danny was there. But her head was spinning, this had her reeling. She still couldn't believe it when she said, 'He was there? What did he do?'

'Played music—they said take your tapes along. Talked to you most of the time. I told him things about you—he asked me. He held your hand. "Come on, Clarry," he said, over and over, night after night. I watched him sweat and I knew he wouldn't be beaten.' Danny smiled faintly then. 'I hadn't got the strength, but he brought you back.'

Those were the echoes in her mind; and the aftershave, the smell of his skin. They said the sense of smell was the first to return, and Nicolas Dargan had been beside her when she was struggling back to life. But not when she regained consciousness. She asked, 'Where was he when I started to come round? Once I was out of the coma, why was that the end of it?'

Perhaps Danny was getting his breath, he was talking more than ever before. Or he could have been deciding to stop here. A few more seconds' silence and she would have been badgering him when he said abruptly, 'Not quite. He paid.'

'Paid for what?'

'For what you needed. My savings soon ran out— I never had more than a few hundred. He backed the business.'

So Nicolas Dargan was her anonymous backer. She heard herself mutter ironically, 'He can be generous. He buys people statues.' Danny stared and she said, 'Sorry, that's something else. Why did he do all this?'

'Challenge,' said Danny promptly, as if he had worked that out long ago. 'He likes a fight. They said you might not wake up. He said you would.'

And luckily for her Nicolas Dargan was a winner.

'And the money?'

'He could afford it,' said Danny. 'Next to nothing to him.'

All the same she wished that money had not been involved. Although without it her business might not have got off the ground, and how the heck did she think that Danny, who never earned that much and never bothered about cash, had saved thousands?

Tight-lipped Danny could certainly keep a secret. Although after all this she would have expected him to be grateful to Nicolas Dargan. 'So why do you hate him?' she asked.

'Don't hate him,' said Danny. 'Just didn't want him around you. He was there the first time your eyes opened. That night I was there too. You weren't seeing much, you went right off again, but they said it was the break-through, and that's when I asked him to keep away.'

'*Why*?' demanded Clarry.

'I didn't want you too grateful for what he'd done, getting too fond of another Dargan. There was no future for you with him.'

No future at all. Everybody knew that, but her voice was wistful. 'So you told him that and he walked away?'

'I told him,' said Danny, concentrating on getting this word-for-word accurate, '"She's still sick, and I don't want her depending on you and mistaking it for anything else," and he said, "God, no."'

That could hardly have been more emphatic. The Sleeping Beauty was waking, and Nicolas Dargan was no Prince. The challenge had been to wake her up, not carry her off.

'He made me take the money for you,' Danny said. 'Said if I did he'd keep out of your life. If I didn't he'd take charge himself. We shook hands, and we never met again till we came here. Never wanted to, never saw the need.'

Danny had protected her when she was weak and defenceless, and it had been a cruel trick of fate that had brought her here. Now she was as strong as if she had never had a day's illness in her life but still as vulnerable as ever where Nicolas Dargan was concerned.

She dabbed her cheeks with her fingertips. The tears were drying, although her throat and head ached with unshed tears. What Danny had told her explained a lot, but there was no comfort in it, and she said huskily, 'I wish we hadn't come back. I'll have to get away.'

'We'll go in the morning,' Danny said.

'I just blew the contract anyway.' Now she was trying to smile again. 'You go to bed. It's been a long day—you look tired.' He looked burned out, and although it was not yet his usual bedtime he got to his feet, still watching her with worried eyes.

'I'll be fine,' Clarry said. She went upstairs with him, and at her bedroom door she said, 'Thank heaven for you, Danny.'

'I couldn't have got you back,' he said.

She owed Nicolas Dargan her sanity and maybe her life, but she had only been a challenge for him. He had never wanted anything from her, except now that she should keep away from Nigel. Well, she could do that for him, Nigel meant nothing to her. And she must keep away from Nicolas too, because he meant something that was tearing her apart.

She could not sleep in this house tonight, where Nicolas might be with Fiona. Tomorrow she would collect Danny and the equipment and leave King's Lodge for ever, but tonight she would rather sleep under a hedge.

She dragged off the red dress and got into jeans and jumper and a jacket, rammed a nightdress and toothbrush into a bag, and went out to the van. There were pubs, hotels where she could get a room for the night. She had to put space between herself and Nicolas Dargan, for she was nearly crazy enough to go looking for him because she couldn't keep away from him.

When she neared the van and saw the faint glimmer of the headlamps she stopped dead and swore fervently at her own carelessness. She had forgotten to switch off the lights, and she knew before she turned the ignition key that the battery was flat and there would be no answering spark to start the engine. She clicked the key a few times, getting nothing; the van was a non-runner unless somebody jump-started it for her, and that would cause fuss and questions.

She could set off walking to the village pub, but she didn't know if they did overnight accommodation, and it was lateish and dark to be walking the lanes. Or she could ring for a taxi. With luck nobody would bother her. She would phone and then she would stand by the gates and wait.

The only person in the hall was Nigel. He was carrying a small case. Clarry said, 'Are you off tonight? Will you give me a lift?'

He looked flushed and dishevelled, as if he too had packed in a hurry, and he wanted to know, 'Where are you going?'

'To the first hotel.'

'Are you sure? There's no need for that.'

'I think there is,' she said, and he shrugged.

'Right, then.'

Clarry walked out of the house with him, collected her bag from the van, and joined him while he was fumbling for the keys to his own white Porsche. His hands were unsteady, and she wondered if he had had further words with Nicolas, whose temper would hardly have been improved by her performance just now.

He was driving slowly and carefully, although the winding lanes were probably safer after dark when you could see the warning lights of oncoming vehicles. When they were well clear of the house he started, 'I'm sorry about everything, but——' and she said quickly,

'Nigel, please shut up. I've just heard how much I owe the Dargans.' He looked blank at that, and she realised that he probably did not know the part Nicolas had played in her recovery nor his investment in her business. She went on, 'But I don't want to talk and I don't want to be talked to. I just want to be put down where I can get a bed for tonight.'

'You've become very hard,' Nigel said huffily, and that was rich coming from him. She looked away from him, through the window, seeing nothing, until ten minutes later when the car turned into a car park fronting a small hotel called the Leaping Salmon, with 'Open to Non-Residents' on the board.

'Will this do?' he asked. Off season they should have a room, and he reached for her bag. 'I'll see you in.'

Background music was playing as they entered the lounge and there were enough customers to give a cheerful atmosphere, although there were empty chairs. Nigel went on ahead to a small reception counter, and Clarry waited until he came back. 'They can fix you up,' he said, and signalled a passing waitress. 'I might as well have one for the road while I'm here.'

She saw then what she should have spotted before if she had been paying him any attention, that he was already over the drink-and-drive limit, and she said, 'A pot of coffee, please,' when the girl reached them. Then she took Nigel's arm and led him to a couple of window seats and an empty table and asked, 'How much have you had already?'

Three of them had shared that bottle of wine over dinner, but he admitted, 'I needed a brandy after that scene with Cole.' At least a couple of doubles, she guessed, and was glad she had hitched a lift with him because he would have been a menace on the busy roads. She knew all about drunk drivers; one had caused the crash that killed her parents.

The coffee came, and she poured two black and sipped some herself. When she had known him he had not been a heavy drinker and no one here would have said he was drunk now, but he certainly should not be driving, which landed her with the problem.

After a flash of irritation she managed to say quietly, 'I can't let you drive, you know.'

'What do you mean?'

'Nigel, you're way over the limit.'

'Do you think so?' He thought about it himself. 'I suppose I could be on the borderline.'

'Shall we go back?' she suggested. 'I could drive your car.'

'*No!*' That panicked him. 'I'm not facing him again tonight. I'm not up to it.'

Clarry smiled ruefully. 'Are you ever? I'll see about another room here.'

'I'll do it.'

As he stood up she said, 'Another single, of course, don't get any silly ideas,' and he rushed to reassure her.

'No danger there. Cole's a mind-reader, I tell you—he'd know.'

As he threaded his way between the chairs across to the booking counter she looked out into the well lit car park. She watched several cars drive out and one drive in, parking beside Nigel's white car. She watched the man get out as Nigel sat down again beside her and said, 'That's done,' and started to pour himself another coffee.

Then she gulped and croaked, 'Drink it quick! Nicolas is just coming across the car park.'

CHAPTER EIGHT

'YOU'RE joking!' Nigel hoped Clarry was, but knew from her expression that she was not. All the same he said, 'I don't believe it.'

I hope you did make it two single rooms, she thought, and knew that that wouldn't prove a thing. Nigel was muttering as if it spooked him, 'How did he know we were here?' and she tried to sound flippant.

'He's not just a mind-reader, he's got a tracker mind as well,' although that was easily explained. If anyone at King's Lodge had heard her mention 'the first hotel' this was it; and Nigel's car was conspicuous in the car park; just following them Nicolas could have spotted it. And that was when he walked into the lounge.

Heads turned as he did. Some here recognised him, some did not, but everyone seemed aware of him. He saw Clarry at once, although the table by the window was in an alcove of its own, and he came towards her without looking away.

At the table he said, 'May I join you?' asking Clarry.

'Do we have a choice?' she asked.

'No.'

'Then be my guest.'

He took an empty chair, still speaking to Clarry, demanding, 'What exactly are you playing at?'

'Don't worry,' she said, 'we're not eloping.'

Nigel tried to say something, but Nicolas overrode him, 'I'm relieved to hear that.' He didn't look relieved. He still looked grim as a hanging judge, and Clarry had done nothing to deserve this and she was not in the happiest of moods herself.

'But you still want an explanation?' She gave him glare for glare. 'All right, and you can believe it or not, because I'm past caring. I'm here because I'd outstayed my welcome in your house and I couldn't get the van to start, so I asked Nigel for a lift. You'd practically thrown him out, hadn't you? Anyhow, I've got a room, and if you ask over there you'll find that he has too, because I've just realised he's in no state to be driving.'

Briefly Nicolas turned his attention on Nigel, who squirmed in his seat. Then he looked back at Clarry, expression and voice heavily ironic. 'That was observant of you. You're taking good care of him.'

'Two singles.'

Nigel got that in, and Nicolas drawled, 'You think that preserves the proprieties?'

'I don't give a damn about the proprieties,' Clarry said hotly, 'and single means single. You didn't have to chase after us.'

'Well, he certainly needs time to sleep it off, and here should do as well as anywhere.' Nicolas was still looking at Clarry, talking to her. 'But I would prefer you back at King's Lodge.'

'Don't you trust me with him? Do you think I might have nightmares again?' He had to be remembering, and suddenly her throat was tight and aching and she had to force out the words, asking Nigel sarcastically, 'Are they adjoining rooms, by the way?'

Nigel was lost, all this was beyond him. What nightmares? What was Clarry on about?

She realised for the first time that the music was sounding louder because those around had stopped talking and joking and were trying to eavesdrop. And she knew that whatever she said or did she would end up leaving with Nicolas. Nigel was talking, but his words were as hazy as the background music.

Nicolas looked across at her steadily, and she could hear, 'Come on, Clarry,' and feel his hand gripping her hand, although they both sat silent and apart.

Then he indicated the small bag. 'Is this yours?' She nodded, and he picked it up and she stood up as he did.

'You'll stay here overnight?' she said to Nigel.

'He will,' said Nicolas grimly.

'Sure,' said Nigel. 'Don't mind me. I'm beginning to think I'm drunk.'

As she drove away in the car beside Nicolas Clarry said, 'It seems I owe you cash, among other things.'

'Who told you that?'

'Danny.'

'You surprise me,' he said drily. 'I got the impression he'd have killed to keep it from you.'

'He was shocked into talking.' Her tears had devastated poor Danny. 'He hasn't changed his mind, but he talked.'

'And he doesn't do much of that.'

'He talked to you in hospital, didn't he?' she pursued. 'Told you things about me.'

'Using very few words.'

'Anyhow, I'll pay you back.' She meant the cash, it was not so easy repaying someone for saving your sanity.

'No need,' he said, but she insisted.

'I shall.'

Lights were burning in windows in King's Lodge and she was sure almost everyone in the house knew that Nicolas had gone after Nigel and the Rickard girl, and the sound of his returning car would have them all straining to hear what was happening. But it seemed like an empty house when they entered the hall. Doors were ajar, but nobody peered out.

They walked up the staircase, and on the first landing Nicolas took her arm and turned her towards the King's Room. When she tried to pull back he said with the same weariness he had shown after her tirade on the lawn, 'You fought me in your coma, most of the time since you've been fighting me—for God's sake let us have a little peace!'

That hushed her for the moment, but when they reached the door she hesitated again, and he said, 'What's the matter now?'

'It will be rather awkward if Fiona's in your bed,' she said wryly.

'That's most unlikely.' He sounded emphatic, although she would have thought there was a very good chance.

Lights were on, but the room was empty and the coverlet of the King's bed was unruffled. Nicolas said, 'Please sit down.'

The chairs in here were old, with flat wooden seats and high backs, valuable antiques but not very comfortable. As Clarry perched herself on one he crossed the room to stand by the fireplace. Then he said, 'I apologise for the scene over dinner. I don't often lose my temper.'

The cracking of an iron self-control had been, as Fiona had said, terrifying. But Fiona had found it a turn-on, and Clarry said tartly, 'Fiona was thrilled. She just loves masterful men.' She was sounding feline and jealous, and she went on quickly, 'But you frightened Nigel half to death. He needed a stiff brandy afterwards.'

'It brought you out in his defence.' She *had* felt sorry for Nigel, she still did, but when Nicolas asked, 'How do you feel about him?' she said:

'I'm no threat to his marriage. If that hits the rocks it won't be through me.'

'Good.' He smiled, for what seemed the first time in a very long while, and again it took the harshness from his face.

'Although it seems tough,' she said, 'keeping them together because Dargan Enterprises needs her father's business.'

'Nigel told you that?'

'Yes.'

He sounded amused. 'Not nearly as much as they need us.'

'Then why did you choose her for him?' Clarry queried.

'Why should I choose her?' This was still amusing him. 'I'm not a marriage broker.'

She leaned forward, staring up at him, bewildered. 'But he said—— I'm sure he did, when he came that last time, you'd sent him to Brussels to keep him away from me, and I asked him if there was anyone else and he said there was this girl you'd more or less chosen for him?' Her voice rose, making that a question, and Nicolas had stopped smiling.

Now he said, 'Listen to me,' which was unnecessary advice when she was hanging on to every word. 'You may not like this, but you have to hear it. The reason Nigel kept away after your accident was because he couldn't face what the future might hold. He asked to be posted overseas.'

This would have shattered her if she had loved Nigel, but she was more concerned with asking Nicolas, 'You didn't send him? You didn't make him go?'

'No, I did not. But nor did I try to change his mind. He would have given you no support. I'm fond of him, but any sign of real trouble and Nigel gives up. Abroad or in the next town it would have been the same. He wouldn't have been around.'

That summed Nigel up, a charmer, a weakling who had soon failed her and then tried to shift the blame.

'Why did *you* come?' she asked.

'I felt responsible for you.'

His horse had thrown her, his kin had deserted her. He had broad shoulders for carrying the load, and she said huskily, 'I'm glad I didn't know.' She had been a case for charity, but it didn't do much for her pride. 'I must have looked a wreck.'

'You looked very small and very hurt. And there was this old man sitting by your bed with tears pouring down his face.'

'Danny doesn't cry,' she said stupidly.

'He cried for you.'

'So you promised him you'd get me back.'

'I promised him. And myself.'

'Thank you.' That was inadequate, and he smiled again.

'You didn't always think it was such a good idea. You weren't that anxious to rejoin the human race.'

'I opened my eyes when you were there?' asked Clarry.

'Several times. The last time you were waking.'

'After that Danny asked you to stay away?'

'What he said seemed reasonable. The last thing I wanted was gratitude. You were recovering, you had your friends.'

'But I didn't have *you*.' The words exploded in her brain like a blinding revelation. Nicolas crossed the room, coming closer to her, and she jumped up, her voice shrill and accusing. 'Damn you, you should have been there—I needed you, I was looking for *you*! Not for Nigel, I hardly ever thought of Nigel again, but you were never out of my mind. You were the one I needed, you were the one who was missing.'

When there was a tapping on the door neither moved. When it came again, light but persistent, Nicolas answered it, opening the door and saying curtly, 'I want nothing, except not to be disturbed again.'

He closed the door and locked it. 'Mrs Haines,' he said. 'Any message for the outside world?' Clarry shook her head, 'I should have come back,' he said, coming to her now, and she said fervently,

'I wish I could have opened my eyes and seen you beside me.'

'So you can.' He smoothed down her eyelids with the gentlest of touches, then picked her up and carried her to the bed. She lay there for a moment, eyes closed. She could have been anywhere, but she was conscious of him. She could smell the faint aftershave, the coolness of his skin. She could feel his breath and hear the beat of a heart that could have been his or her own.

Then he said, 'Clarry,' and her eyelids were heavy as if she was waking from a deep sleep. She saw him muzzily at first through her long lashes, then so clearly that if she had never seen him again she would have remembered how she was seeing him now when she was old.

Crazily, she was weak. She could hardly lift her head, and her lips were so dry that her voice was faint, but thankfulness swept over her because he was here, where he should have been after he had called her back from the shadows. 'Hold me,' she whispered, and he held her close, cradling her, until she felt his strength in her blood.

'Don't leave me,' she said, as she would have said nearly two years ago.

'I won't,' he promised.

For a while all she needed was having his arms around her. If he had been there for her, during the long haul of her recovery and the dark nightmares, she would never have been afraid. She asked, 'If Danny hadn't asked you to stay away, would you have come back?'

'Yes, I would.' She believed him. She would always believe him, because she knew in her heart that he would never lie to her.

'Then he's got a lot to answer for,' she said. 'I was so angry with you. I felt you'd cheated me.'

She lay in the curve of his arm, looking up at him. 'I was cheated too,' he said. 'I hadn't seen you smile. I waited for that and then I missed it.' She smiled for him, her senses swimming, seeing something in his eyes that turned her bones molten. 'Danny couldn't tell me what I wanted to know,' he said. 'How your voice sounded, how you laughed and moved.'

It was hard to believe that when he walked away for the last time she had not called after him, 'Come back!' She said, 'I wasn't doing anything much then, was I?'

'At first you were in some faraway place where nobody could reach you.'

He would always reach her, no matter how far away she was, and she said, 'Danny said I was a challenge for you. You said you'd get me back and you wouldn't be beaten.'

'That might have been how it started, but before long it was like life or death.' She could have been trapped in the limbo of a living death, but he said, 'Mine,' and she gasped at that. 'I had a compartmentalised mind, I could function as usual professionally, but whenever I could get away I went back to you. It was as if you'd always been very dear to me and your recovery would be the best thing that could ever happen.'

Clarry was so glad he had felt like that. That some time she had been the best thing. She nestled very close and she loved the sound of his deep voice. She could lie here for ever, just listening to him.

He said, 'Then he talked about you being too grateful and I realised I was getting too possessive. He loves you, your "grandfather", he wanted you to have the chance of living your own life, and I felt that he must know you best.'

She shot upright. 'Well, he *didn't*!' Her vehemence made him smile.

'At least he was a disinterested party. He wanted nothing for himself.'

'What did you want?' she asked.

He still held her, and she looked at him and wanted him more than she had ever wanted anything or anyone.

He said, 'I wanted to see you getting stronger, hear your secrets, buy you presents, take you places.' The tenderness in his voice and his smile made her the richest woman in the world. 'Get into your mind,' he said, 'steal your soul, watch your hair grow.' He stroked along the silver streak and she felt that the tendrils of her hair must be curling and clinging around his finger.

She laughed softly. 'Where would have been the harm in that?' Of course there would have been danger, but she would willingly have paid any price, and she teased, 'But you gave up on me.'

'I always knew how you were making out,' he told her.

'*Did* you fix it for us to come here?'

'No, the Mountjoys did me a favour there without realising it. But I would have engineered a meeting before long. It was high time.'

Nearly two years was a long time, and in her ignorance she could have kept away from him for ever. She wondered, 'If Danny hadn't told me what happened would you have told me?'

'Eventually. I hoped you might remember.'

'I do remember.' Nicolas had always been in her subconscious, under her skin. Now the confusion had cleared from her mind she could recapture her dream images and recognise the face she had looked for when she woke. But then she was a caricature of today's glowing girl, and she asked, fishing shamelessly for compliments, 'How did I turn out?'

He grinned. 'Much as I expected, all spark and spirit.'

Showing too much spirit at times. Clarry pulled a contrite face. 'Sorry about some of the things I said. They must have made you consider dumping me again.'

'There were times when I thought, I don't need this.' She held her breath. 'But I did,' he said. 'I do.'

'*You* need *me*?'

That was what he had just said, but she wanted to hear it again. 'I need you,' he said. His voice was rough and urgent, and a slow fire was creeping through her, making her gasp for breath. The clothes she wore were heavy, suffocating. Her coat dragged her down and she fumbled with buttons, getting it open.

Her fingers were thumbs, and when his hands took over she said, 'Thank you,' as if he was helping her out of a raincoat rather than stripping her to the skin. His hands were trembling too, she felt their unsteadiness, and she tried to make it easier. If she had stayed in the red dress she could have been out of that in no time, but now she had to squirm down from the sweater he was pulling over her head and out of her jeans. Fever would consume her if she didn't get cool air to her body, and her bra straps slipped and the fastener was tricky, and he tore it apart and as it fell from her she gasped, 'Turn out the lights.'

'Why?'

She looked down at herself and wondered when her shoes had come off and her tights, and said,

'I'm not that gorgeous,' as if she was looking at herself for the first time.

'Oh, yes, you are,' he said.

She was on fire for him. Nothing else would assuage the agony that was raging through her, and he kissed the leaping pulse in her throat and his lips never left her skin, and she closed her eyes as the light kisses ran over her.

When he was naked above her, the lines of a John Donne poem she had learned long ago were almost her last rational thought... 'If ever any beauty I did see which I desired and got, 'twas but a dream of thee...'

After that she was beyond reason and into an orgy of uncaring bliss, where everything happening to her was sending her wild. She revelled in every inch of her body and his, the slow, sensuous build-up had her moaning, and his mouth was covering hers and her tongue writhed and fought and tempted like a snake.

This was lust and love, and she trusted him so that she held back in no way, giving all that she had to give and letting the incredible pleasure he was giving her soak into every pore, fuelling the white heat until the volcanic conclusion sent her higher than heaven but still clinging to him. He was holding her together as she burned and soared, and falling she knew that she screamed, or laughed, or both, and hardly knew if she was living or dying.

She came round wondering if she *had* passed out, because she was under the coverlets now, snug in the bed. Nicolas lay beside her looking down at her as if he had been waiting for her to open her eyes, and this was how she always wanted it to be, waking to find him here, taking her naked body in his naked arms.

It wouldn't always happen, she knew that, but it did now, and she had experienced such joy through his hands, through all of him, that echoes of ecstasy were still throbbing in her heartbeats and her pulses.

She was spoiled for any other man's lovemaking. She would never find another lover like him, and she pressed her face against his chest, the dark hairs tickling her nose, and heard herself sigh. 'Fiona said you were sensational.'

'Sensational at what?'

'Well——' she raised her head and wished she hadn't said that '—this, I suppose.'

'That's flattering.' It was making him smile. 'Especially as we never got beyond the platonic.'

'Are you sure?' she asked, and giggled at the daftness of that, and because she was high on happiness.

'Are you suggesting I don't know the difference between platonic and this?' The giggles took over as he held her, squeezing the breath out of her, so close that they fitted perfectly and she could feel him against every inch of her.

So it had been wishful thinking, wishful hoping on Fiona's part. Nicolas said, 'It's King's Lodge that Miss Stretton lusts after.'

And the status that went with it, although Clarry was sure of her facts when she teased breathlessly, 'Believe me, she lusts after you, especially when you're bullying poor Nigel. Don't you fancy her? She's a very classy lady?'

'Very classy,' he said solemnly. 'Well up in the well-dressed lists. But I never had the slightest urge to tear her clothes off.' His hand stroked Clarry lightly, sending little shivers of delight through her, while he talked on.

'When I bought the house it was obvious that Fiona Stretton could come with it, and I was surprised to find that the offer didn't appeal to me. It had been some time since I'd found any woman particularly engrossing, but she could have been an exception. Physically. Mentally she's a boring little snob. But physically she's attractive enough, and she was available, and she left me cold.

'Just as others had. They all seemed to lack something. I couldn't have said what it was and I didn't know where to look for it, until last month when I saw a woman walking down Regent Street. Her hair was loose and dark and she was wearing a yellow coat and hurrying so that a yellow scarf flew out behind her. Before I caught up with her I saw that she was a stranger, but at first I'd thought that she might have been you.

'I'd always taken it for granted that we should meet again, walk into the same room somewhere or come face to face in some town. But after the woman in Regent Street I'd waited long enough. I wasn't leaving it to chance any longer. I had to see you again, and soon. You'd look different, of course, but I'd recognise you, although I was almost sure you wouldn't know me. But I had to find out if what I'd felt for you when I walked away from your bed could have grown into something a great deal stronger. If you could be the reason other women wouldn't do.'

With a half laugh he said, 'When I saw Rickard Restoration suggested for repairs I got back to King's Lodge and waited for you.'

'And found me, lying on the King's bed.' Opening her eyes and seeing him, almost remembering. Clarry said huskily, 'What you felt then had grown?'

'As though we'd never been apart. From the first day I had a hell of a job keeping my hands off you.'

'That's nice.' She ran fingertips over his face, tracing the off-centre bone of the hooked nose, touching the strong sensual mouth, thinking what a feeble word 'nice' was to describe the bliss of knowing that she could roam anywhere, that this man's body was her kingdom as hers was his. 'So why didn't you stay with me after the storm?' she asked.

'I might have thought I'd be taking an unfair advantage.'

'Oh, no.' She shook her head. 'I don't buy that; that wouldn't have stopped you. Didn't you want to?'

'Of course I wanted you. So badly that if I'd stayed I'd have been committed. You might not have been, but I would, and that was on my mind all the way back here. Then there was Danny waiting for us, loathing my guts for what he saw as my double-dealing—we'd had a gentleman's agreement that I'd keep out of your life—and I knew how much influence he has on you.'

'Oh, Danny's a gentleman all right, but no one alive has that much influence. He didn't think you'd be good for me, and he's wrong there.' She laughed softly with dancing eyes, 'Because there isn't any of me you're not good for.'

'Tell him that, will you?' Nicolas's grin was wicked. 'No need to go into specifics! But if you could bring him round eventually to considering me as a grandson that would make me very happy.'

There was no laughter in his eyes, and her smile stiffened as she stammered, 'What did you say?'

'I'm asking his granddaughter to marry me.'

She heard herself blurting, 'Nigel said you weren't a marrying man.'

'My darling idiot, Nigel knows nothing about anything, so he can have no idea how I feel about you. Out in the garden he was asking, "What have I done?" and I couldn't explain that I was so bloody jealous finding you and him looking like lovers again that I nearly threw him across the room. What I did say was "Get out of my sight," and that was unreasonable when I'd just ordered him outside to talk.'

'Poor Nigel!' Now Clarry had to smile when she pitied Nigel. 'No wonder he needed all that brandy! You didn't really think we'd gone off together?'

'You had. No, I couldn't believe you were together, except as travelling companions, but I had to get you back, because when you're not around nothing seems to have much purpose. I love you, nothing I do or amount to will give me any satisfaction unless I can share it with you. So, will you marry me, because I don't seem able to face the prospect of living without you?'

She couldn't understand why he was pleading so desperately, because she thought she had said yes. She slid her warm bare arms around him, her hands behind his head, her fingers deep in his thick dark hair. 'Of course I'll marry you,' she said. 'Of course I will. Don't ever leave me again.'

'I never did,' he said, and it was the truth. They had been together ever since he first held her hand in pity, and they would belong to each other in passion and tenderness and never-failing love through all the years of their lives.

EXPERIENCE THE EXOTIC

VISIT . . . INDONESIA, TUNISIA, EGYPT AND MEXICO . . . THIS SUMMER

Enjoy the experience of exotic countries with our Holiday Romance Pack

Four exciting new romances by favourite Mills & Boon authors.

Available from July 1993   Price: £7.20

Mills & Boon

*Available from W.H. Smith, John Menzies, Martins, Forbuoys, most supermarkets and other paperback stockists.
Also available from Mills & Boon Reader Service, FREEPOST, PO Box 236, Thornton Road, Croydon, Surrey CR9 9EL.
(UK Postage & Packaging free)*

Another Face...
Another Identity...
Another Chance...

When her teenage love turns to hate, Geraldine Frances vows to even the score. After arranging her own "death", she embarks on a dramatic transformation emerging as *Silver*, a hauntingly beautiful and mysterious woman few men would be able to resist.

With a new face and a new identity, she is now ready to destroy the man responsible for her tragic past.

Silver – a life ruled by one all-consuming passion, is Penny Jordan at her very best.

WORLDWIDE

Available from W.H. Smith, John Menzies, Martins, Forbuoys, most supermarkets and other paperback stockists.

Also available from Mills and Boon Reader Service, Freepost, P.O. Box 236, Thornton Road, Croydon, Surrey CR9 9EL

£3.99

4 FREE
Romances and 2 FREE gifts just for you!

You can enjoy all the heartwarming emotion of true love for FREE! Discover the heartbreak and happiness, the emotion and the tenderness of the modern relationships in Mills & Boon Romances.

We'll send you 4 Romances as a special offer from Mills & Boon Reader Service, along with the opportunity to have 6 captivating new Romances delivered to your door each month.

Claim your FREE books and gifts overleaf...

An irresistible offer from Mills & Boon

Become a regular reader of Romances with Mills & Boon Reader Service and we'll welcome you with 4 books, a CUDDLY TEDDY and a special MYSTERY GIFT all absolutely FREE.

And then look forward to receiving 6 brand new Romances each month, delivered to your door hot off the presses, postage and packing FREE! Plus our free Newsletter featuring author news, competitions, special offers and much more.

This invitation comes with no strings attached. You may cancel or suspend your subscription at any time, and still keep your free books and gifts.

It's so easy. Send no money now. Simply fill in the coupon below and post it to -
Reader Service, FREEPOST, PO Box 236, Croydon, Surrey CR9 9EL.

NO STAMP REQUIRED

Free Books Coupon

Yes! Please rush me 4 FREE Romances and 2 FREE gifts! Please also reserve me a Reader Service subscription. If I decide to subscribe I can look forward to receiving 6 brand new Romances for just £10.80 each month, postage and packing FREE. If I decide not to subscribe I shall write to you within 10 days - I can keep the free books and gifts whatever I choose. I may cancel or suspend my subscription at any time. I am over 18 years of age.

Ms/Mrs/Miss/Mr _____ EP56R

Address _____

_____

Postcode _____ Signature _____

Offers closes 31st March 1994. The right is reserved to refuse an application and change the terms of this offer. This offer does not apply to Romance subscribers. One application per household. Overseas readers please write for details. Southern Africa write to Book Services International Ltd., Box 41654, Craighall, Transvaal 2024. You may be mailed with offers from other reputable companies as a result of this application. Please tick box if you would prefer not to receive such offers. ☐

mps MAILING PREFERENCE SERVICE

Mills & Boon

Forthcoming Titles

DUET
Available in June

The Carole Mortimer Duet — **VELVET PROMISE** / **TANGLED HEARTS**

The Sally Wentworth Duet — **MISTAKEN WEDDING** / **SATAN'S ISLAND**

BEST SELLER ROMANCE
Available in July

THE COURSE OF TRUE LOVE Betty Neels
STORM CLOUD MARRIAGE Roberta Leigh

MEDICAL ROMANCE
Available in July

JUST WHAT THE DOCTOR ORDERED Caroline Anderson
LABOUR OF LOVE Janet Ferguson
THE FAITHFUL TYPE Elizabeth Harrison
A CERTAIN HUNGER Stella Whitelaw

Available from W.H. Smith, John Menzies, Martins, Forbuoys, most supermarkets and other paperback stockists.

Also available from Mills & Boon Reader Service, Freepost, P.O. Box 236, Thornton Road, Croydon, Surrey CR9 9EL.

Readers in South Africa - write to:
Book Services International Ltd, P.O. Box 41654, Craighall, Transvaal 2024.

Next Month's Romances

Each month you can choose from a wide variety of romance with Mills & Boon. Below are the new titles to look out for next month, why not ask either Mills & Boon Reader Service or your Newsagent to reserve you a copy of the titles you want to buy – just tick the titles you would like and either post to Reader Service or take it to any Newsagent and ask them to order your books.

Please save me the following titles:	Please tick	✓
THE SEDUCTION OF KEIRA	Emma Darcy	
THREAT FROM THE PAST	Diana Hamilton	
DREAMING	Charlotte Lamb	
MIRRORS OF THE SEA	Sally Wentworth	
LAWFUL POSSESSION	Catherine George	
DESIGNED TO ANNOY	Elizabeth Oldfield	
A WOMAN ACCUSED	Sandra Marton	
A LOVE LIKE THAT	Natalie Fox	
LOVE'S DARK SHADOW	Grace Green	
THE WILLING CAPTIVE	Lee Stafford	
MAN OF THE MOUNTAINS	Kay Gregory	
LOVERS' MOON	Valerie Parv	
CRUEL ANGEL	Sharon Kendrick	
LITTLE WHITE LIES	Marjorie Lewty	
PROMISE ME LOVE	Jennifer Taylor	
LOVE'S FANTASY	Barbara McMahon	

If you would like to order these books in addition to your regular subscription from Mills & Boon Reader Service please send £1.80 per title to: Mills & Boon Reader Service, Freepost, P.O. Box 236, Croydon, Surrey, CR9 9EL, quote your Subscriber No:................................. (If applicable) and complete the name and address details below. Alternatively, these books are available from many local Newsagents including W.H.Smith, J.Menzies, Martins and other paperback stockists from 9th July 1993.

Name:...
Address:..
....Post Code:........................

To Retailer: If you would like to stock M&B books please contact your regular book/magazine wholesaler for details.

You may be mailed with offers from other reputable companies as a result of this application.
If you would rather not take advantage of these opportunities please tick box ☐